THE VANISHING TROPHIES

THE QUICK-WITTED QUADRUPLETS

ISHAAN CHOPRA

ISBN
Paperback 979-8-89322-603-4
Hardcase 979-8-89588-946-6

Contents

Acknowledgement

I want to thank my mother and my father who agreed to my idea of writing a book and helped me find the right publisher to publish this book. My book would not have been a reality without them.

I also want to thank my twin brother, Vivaan Chopra, who motivated me, while writing his own book.

A special thanks to my teachers at Bishop Cotton Boys' School who taught me the language and the vocabulary that I have used in this book. I also want to express my gratitude to the Roots Football Club that has provided me the confidence and also taught me how to manage many things at the same time.

My sincere thanks to Ms Priyanka Reddy for the wonderful cover design and illustrations for my book.

Chapter - 1

The Mayor's Call

It was a nice sunny morning on a beautiful summer day with the pleasant sound of the birds chirping. Suddenly, there was a loud banging on the door of Jack and Zack. Both the boys were fast asleep in their room, so it took them some time to wake up.

Jack and Zack were surprised and nervous with such a loud knock at their door so early in the morning. They quickly picked up their tennis rackets as a matter of caution and headed towards the door slowly and quietly. Silently, they opened the door and heard two voices that frightened them and made Jack slip on the doormat.

The people who knocked on the door were none other than Bryan and Ryan, close friends of Jack and Zack.

The visitors helped Jack get up and asked him if he was alright. Jack seemed to be fine and quickly came back to his feet feeling embarrassed.

Ryan told them, "Late last night, we got a message from the mayor's office. The mayor wants to honour both of you, along with a few others. The event will take place after about ten days as part of a special ceremony."

Bryan added enthusiastically, "It is a very prestigious year for our county, and the tournaments held recently are a part of special celebrations marking the centenary year of the county. This is why the mayor wants to honour the players. Remember, the county of Kent was founded several hundred years ago. In a few days, our county celebrates another centenary."

Zack replied irritably, "Both of you don't remember what happened to us?"

Jack further added, "We will make a fool of ourselves on that day when the mayor will call us on the stage to honour us."

The pair of twins, Jack and Zack, were woken
up by their close twin friends, Bryan and Ryan. Together, they
were known as the *Quadruplets*.

There was silence in the room for a few minutes as the boys remembered everything. Then suddenly, Ryan declared, "Jack and Zack, we have no choice now. You both have to meet the mayor on the day you have been invited."

Both Jack and Zack replied together in a sad voice, "But we are just not ready to meet the mayor. You know what a terrible thing has happened to us." Jack further added, "We have not told anyone about it, and that's good. If we tell people, they will make fun of us and call us the Careless Team."

Then Bryan and Ryan almost said in the same voice, "Maybe we can get it back; we still have some time. We have to make you ready to meet the mayor." Bryan added, "Come, let's all go down to the dining hall to have breakfast while we discuss what to do next."

Jack and Zack were eleven-year-old twin boys who were good tennis players and had been invited by the mayor at the county's centenary celebrations.

Bryan and Ryan were also a pair of twins, slightly older, around thirteen years of age. The four boys had always been together and were known as the *'quadruplets'*. It used to take a long time to convince people that they were not siblings. Even their friends initially thought the four boys were brothers. Even though most of the boys in the school had found out they were not siblings, they were still known as quadruplets.

All the four boys lived in Canterbury, a small city in the county of Kent, England. Kent borders Greater London and is known as the 'Garden of England' for having many orchards and gardens. They were all going to the same school – Palmers Green High School. Their summer vacations had just started, but all four boys were staying at the school dormitory for a few days so that they could practice and participate in tournaments.

Jack was a fair complexioned boy with dark brown hair, which looked like black hair. He had a European round-shaped face and brown eyes. His height was four feet ten inches.

Zack, Jack's twin brother, was also a fair complexioned boy with blond hair. He had an oval-shaped face and brown eyes. His height was slightly less than his twin brother – four feet nine inches.

Ryan and Bryan were identical twins. They were fair-complexioned boys with light brown hair. Both of them had oval-shaped faces and blue eyes, and their height was five feet one inch.

Chapter - 2

The Tournament

At the breakfast table of the school's dining hall, the four boys reflected on the series of events, which transpired in the last few days from the time when Jack and Zack won everything and yet lost everything.

It all began on a Saturday morning a few weeks ago when the tennis coach, Chris Wilson, asked Jack and Zack if they would like to participate in a prestigious local tennis tournament – The Kent County Centenary Tournament. Teams from all the main cities and towns of the county of Kent, including Canterbury, were participating in this tournament. Jack and Zack had an opportunity to represent their city of Canterbury, as they had previously done well in the inter-school tournament of the city.

The coach told them that both the twin boys could play in the Doubles Tennis tournament. The coach further explained to them that they were playing well, and they needed to start participating in local county tournaments. Moreover, as the coach pointed out, the tennis tournament was a prestigious local county event as part of the centenary celebrations of the county.

Jack and Zack were hesitant at first, as they were only eleven years old. Their twin friends, Bryan and Ryan, kept on encouraging them by telling them that the tournament would be fun and that Jack and Zack could win it. The praise from their friends encouraged both Jack and Zack, and finally they were ready to play the tournament.

Jack and Zack were nervous on the day of the first match, but they were surprised to see how accurately and nicely they struck the ball. They were facing an easy opponent and, just after the first few points, the boys knew they would win. The game ended when the boys won in two straight sets. The first set was pleasing to the eye, as Jack and Zack did not make any errors and forced the opponents to enable them a 6-2 win. The second set was as bad as the first one for their opponents. The twin boys managed to do even better, and in the second set, they won even more easily than the first set. The second one ended 6-1. The match was won 6-2 and 6-1.

The boys were really happy, as they had won their first game and were in the quarter-finals. The next match was on Wednesday, which was two days away. So, the two boys, along with their friends Bryan and Ryan, decided to have fun. Just as they were about to go for a relaxed afternoon of fun and merry-making, the tennis coach, Chris Wilson, asked the boys where they were headed. Jack said, "Coach, can you please give us permission? We are going to the fair to celebrate our first victory."

The coach seemed not too happy and said, "You think you can take it lightly? Your match is on Wednesday, and you need to practise your serves. Also, I saw you could not run towards the end of the match. You want to know why?" Jack and Zack replied, "Yes coach." "It is because you have less stamina. If you run around the tennis court five times without stopping, I will allow you to go to the fair till evening, but tomorrow, you have to run twelve rounds," the coach replied angrily. Relieved that he was letting them go, Jack and Zack replied, "Fine, coach."

The boys thought they could easily run, but it was harder than they thought. After three rounds, they started to feel tired and thought of stopping. Then they remembered the coach's words that they needed to run five rounds without stopping. They somehow managed to complete five rounds, and the coach was happy. He called them and told, "Now you can enjoy. But no unhealthy food and come back by six in the evening."

Jack and Zack hurried back to their room and changed into their casual clothes and then met Bryan and Ryan, who were eagerly waiting for them. The fair was about a kilometre away from the school and the boys had a good run to reach the fair. Jack joked, "This is why Coach Wilson let us go."

The fair was really crowded and noisy, but exciting. First, the four boys decided to go to the food stalls. Suddenly, they remembered that Jack and Zack could not eat unhealthy food. They went to the amusement rides instead. They got in and were waiting for the ride to start. It looked like the helpers were stopping a lady from taking her ten-month-old child on the ride. It was clearly written on the board near the ride that children under the age of three were not allowed. After the ride, they were really dizzy. Ryan said, "Good thing we didn't eat anything." Zack agreeably said, "Yeah, or else we'd be throwing up." Bryan had a quick glance at his watch and said, "We have just enough time to visit the game stalls." They rushed to the game stalls and started to play darts. Bryan won the game and a squishy trophy.

A quick glance at Bryan's watch got them worried; it seemed that they would be late in reaching back to the school. They should have left the fair a few minutes earlier to reach school on time, as instructed by the coach. They ran as fast as they could. The quadruplets reached twenty-seven seconds before time! They were relieved to find that the coach was not angry. The boys had a quiet supper and retired to bed early. It had been a tiring day for the four boys, and soon they were fast asleep.

They awoke late the next morning. Jack and Zack changed and freshened up in the wink of an eye and hurriedly went to the tennis coach. He angrily said, "This is why I didn't want to send you to the fair, but I did. Now, do your twelve rounds. Thereafter, both of you practise your game for one hour."

The running to the fair and from the fair really gave them confidence and they could do the twelve rounds with ease. The coach said, "Come here again after breakfast."

Jack and Zack went to have their breakfast. They were surprised to see Bryan and Ryan just coming for breakfast, as their friends were usually early risers. Thereafter, all four of them went to the tennis ground. Jack and Zack, helped by Bryan and Ryan, practised some backhand shots followed by a few races. Bryan and Ryan, being older, were faster than Jack and Zack. Bryan won most of the races and Ryan usually came second. The boys found it fun. They were shocked to see how time flew.

It was almost lunch time. After a hurried lunch, Jack and Zack went to their coach for a post lunch session. The coach had called them to tell about their opponents. The coach said, "In the quarter-finals, we face Peter Hendricks and Isaac Hilton. They are known for delicately chipping the ball in front of the net to make it harder for their opponents. You two should stay forward, as they are not good in smashes. They can only chip." They dedicated the next three hours to practising tennis and were exhausted. Thereafter, they went back to their room to relax. The boys had a quiet supper and retired by 6:30 p.m.

Jack and Zack woke up early the next morning and changed quickly into their sports attire, as they had their match scheduled in the day. Just as they opened the door, they got the shock of their lives. Two short men were outside the room and ordered them to eat a quick breakfast and follow them. Both Jack and Zack were scared, but they followed the orders. After a quick breakfast, Jack and Zack nervously followed the two men out into the ground. The men took out their moustaches and wigs, and when they turned around again, Jack and Zack found out they were none other than their friends, Bryan and Ryan. Bryan and Ryan laughed and said, "You really thought we were men. We thought our disguises were bad and you both would recognise us." Jack and Zack were angry, but they soon calmed down.

Jack and Zack went along with Bryan and Ryan to their coach, who was waiting for them. They climbed into the coach's car, and they were off to the quarter-final match. Both Jack and Zack were really worried before the game, but their strategy worked very well, and they won in two straight sets, this time too. This time they won 6-1 and 6-1, unlike 6-2 and 6-1 as in their previous match. Their opponents stood no chance; they never expected young Jack and Zack to play so well. Jack and Zack were happy, as they had won again and thus progressed to the semifinals. Happily, the boys went back to their school.

After eating a more filling breakfast the next day morning at their school, they met their coach, who told them to take the day off to relax.

The boys went to Bryan and Ryan's room and asked them if they could play some fun games. Bryan and Ryan said, "Yes." The quadruplets went to the ground and started playing hide-and-seek. First, Bryan was the seeker, and he took just three minutes to catch Ryan. Ryan searched everywhere but couldn't find the others. Just as he was about to quit, he heard Jack laugh softly. Ryan followed the laugh and caught Jack. In turn, Jack took less than three minutes to catch Zack. After enjoying the game, they went to eat lunch.

After lunch, the quadruplets started playing a game of Ludo. It was a long game with no clear winner, till Jack got a couple of good numbers by rolling the dice. Jack and Zack were tired and had an afternoon nap. They woke up at twelve minutes past four and decided to go to Bryan and Ryan's room.

Surprisingly, the door was locked. They knocked and the door opened. Bryan said, "We are getting ready for the magic show. Want to come?" Jack and Zack hurried back to their room, changed, and came down for the show along with their friends. The show was amazing. The tricks which the magician was doing seemed impossible. After the show, they had dinner, and then they settled with a book each before sleeping. It had been a relaxing and happy day.

The next day when the boys woke up, they freshened up, changed, ate a quick breakfast and then went to the coach, Chris Wilson.

Bryan and Ryan assisted the coach, Chris Wilson, by making sure their friends and doubles players ran twenty rounds. After finishing the twenty rounds, Jack and Zack did some strenuous tennis training and then had their lunch. After lunch, they trained again till it was dark. After the whole day's training, they were exhausted. They somehow managed to have their dinner. Then Jack and Zack went to their room where they talked and talked about many different topics.

Jack and Zack were a bit nervous, as the semi-final was the following day. Even though only Jack and Zack were playing the match, Bryan and Ryan were equally nervous for their friends. Bryan and Ryan thought Jack and Zack would be awake and went to the players' room. Jack and Zack were awake and were surprised to see their friends. Bryan and Ryan gave a few tips to help Jack and Zack calm down the night before the match. They also cheered Jack and Zack to reduce their worries. Jack and Zack were thankful to Bryan and Ryan for the advice and cheers. Then Jack and Zack decided to read a book each, which made them feel sleepy. Their eyelids were drooping, and they were yawning every two minutes. Before they knew it, they were sleeping and dreaming of winning the next day.

Jack and Zack woke up at eighteen minutes past six the next morning and first went to Bryan and Ryan's room, while Bryan and Ryan went to Jack and Zack's room. The two sets of twins were surprised not to see others in their rooms. They all rushed to the hall, looking for the other pair of twins. Jack and Zack were hurrying down the stairs to the hall when two boys ahead of them were slowly going down the stairs, seemingly looking for someone.

Jack finally got so impatient with the pace of the two boys ahead and said irritably, "Hey guys, move. Why are you so slow?" The two boys in front slowly turned around. Jack and Zack were surprised that the two boys blocking them were none other than Bryan and Ryan. All the four boys had a hearty laugh on the whole incident.

The four of them went to their coach, Chris Wilson, who told Bryan and Ryan to cheer the boys on in the important semi-final game. Jack and Zack practised for the match, which was in the evening. The boys played diligently until lunch and then they ate a small and quick bite before going back to coach Chris Wilson, who would then take them to the match. It was a long and quiet drive for around an hour, and by the time they reached, it was already 5:00 p.m. They practised again at the stadium, till it was dark. Finally, it was time to go to the main court for the match. The floodlights made the surface of the court shine, and the crowd cheered as they entered. The boys acknowledged by waving happily to the people around. However, the opponents were late, so Jack and Zack were surprised at what was happening. Finally, the opponents came apologetically, as their car had a puncture on the way. All was set for the semi-final match.

The boys warmed up, and then it was time for the match to commence. A phenomenal performance was exhibited by Jack and Zack, as they won the match 6-3 and 6-2. The first set was one-sided, as Jack and Zack quickly got into the flow of the game and were playing their best. The second set was even better, with both playing their best game ever. The boys were delighted to reach the finals.

In the finals, they would be facing none other than William and Matthew Taylor, the pair of twins who had won last year. William and Matthew held the record of being the youngest doubles champions at the age of twelve years. If Jack and Zack won, they would break the record of William and Matthew by becoming the youngest doubles champions.

The final was on Sunday evening, and they had just Saturday to practice. It was also interesting that the doubles' final match was between two pairs of twins.

After returning to school, Jack and Zack were happy to see the whole school erupting in cheers as they were in the finals. Also, the boys laughed about an all twins' final. The celebration went on for quite some time. The school friends were happy for Jack and Zack, and the teachers allowed them to party till night. By then most of the boys were tired and decided to go to sleep. Some of the boys wanted to party more, but the teachers insisted on sleeping.

Chapter - 3

The Finals

The day before finals, Saturday, was full of practice. The boys diligently started their sessions after eating breakfast and continued up to lunch time. Lunch was a boring and quiet meal, as the boys were thinking of the finals. After lunch, they excitedly practised again. At 5:00 p.m. they were asked by the coach to take a break and relax.

The boys decided to relax by playing hide-and-seek. The first seeker was the clever chap, Zack. He was a boy of intelligence. He searched and saw a movement behind a bush. He walked away from the bush, acting like he did not see anything, and then quickly turned around and ran towards the bush to catch the person behind it. The person caught first was Ryan, and then he also started searching for others.

Ryan searched until he found a large tree. He thought someone would be behind the tree, but to his dismay, there was no one behind the tree. He then saw a patch of heather and lay down next to it. He saw varieties of birds like turtle doves, wood pigeons, parakeets, etc. Still, he was unhappy that he did not catch anyone. Zack, who was hiding nearby, felt pity for Ryan and asked Ryan to catch him. Ryan was touched by Zack's kindness, but refused. The others saw this act of kindness from Zack and came out of their hiding places while clapping. This act of kind-heartedness helped Zack to show that he was a kind person, a true friend, and a person who would care for everyone.

The quadruplets went back to the school hall to have dinner and saw the tennis coach, Chris Wilson. The coach gently came near Jack and Zack and said, "Don't be nervous. Even if you don't win, you'll come second and be crowned as runners-up." Both the boys seemed relaxed, ate a quick dinner, and slept early.

Jack and Zack woke up on the day of the finals on Sunday, freshened up and went to the tennis coach. The tennis coach asked, "Have you eaten your breakfast?" The boys replied, "No." The coach asked them to relax and first eat their breakfast and then come. They ate a quick breakfast and went to the coach, who told them to play a practice match between themselves.

The practice match between Jack and Zack was so entertaining and competitive that each game took about three to five minutes. The first set ended 7-5 to Zack, the second 7-5 to Jack and the third 7-6 to Zack. The practice game ended just before lunch. After that, the boys had a filling lunch as they were hungry and exhausted. They also carried an energy drink each for the finals.

All the four boys went to the tennis coach, who took them in his car to the match venue. They reached well on time and got themselves warmed up for the match. They were waiting for their opponents – William and Matthew Taylor.

Incidentally, William and Matthew were also twin brothers! William was a well-built boy of thirteen years who had gentle eyes and a kind face. His twin brother Matthew was identical to him, and the difference between them was that Matthew was taller by an inch. The crowd of spectators was already screaming and enthusiastically cheering for the double's finalists, and the sound was almost unbearable.

The match was taking place in Woodland Park, London. This court was one of the best tennis courts in England. Even the most prestigious tournaments took place there. The four finalists were happy, as they would be playing on one of the best tennis courts in England.

The players shook hands before the start of the final match. Jack and Zack were happy, as they thought they had a good chance to win against Matthew and William Taylor, just like they won against their opponents in the earlier matches. The match started with the crowd cheering as loud as they could.

The first set was dominated by Matthew and William Taylor. The set was totally one-sided, and Matthew and William won 6-0! Matthew and William controlled the full set, which lasted for just sixteen minutes.

Jack and Zack felt really embarrassed, and they wanted to quit playing the game, as they feared losing 6-0, 6-0 and 6-0.

They went to their coach, who was seated with Bryan and Ryan. Surprisingly, Bryan and Ryan quietly ran out without telling anything, while the coach told the boys, "Matthew and William are thirteen years old, and they are much stronger than you both. I have observed that you are unable to pick their serves and smashes, as you are staying too forward. Go a little back and receive the ball when it is slightly slower, and then hit the ball back softly so it will just bounce on the other side of the net. This will force them to run forward for the ball towards the net, which is difficult. After some games, again change the ball placement to make it more difficult for them. Again, after a few more games, do whatever you want to make it even more unpredictable for the opponent."

The boys understood the coach's instructions, and this time they had a ray of hope to prevent them from losing. They were sad and angry, as their best friends, Bryan and Ryan, had suddenly abandoned them. They took a sip of water, went back towards the court, and then it struck them. They could win this game, but to achieve it they needed to put in extraordinary efforts.

Just as the game was restarting, they felt that the cheer for them was suddenly much louder. They thought that they must be imagining it, but they still looked and saw Bryan and Ryan playing a drum to cheer them on. They felt happy that Bryan and Ryan were doing their best to encourage them. It gave Jack and Zack lots of confidence.

Jack and Zack started to implement their coach's strategy, and it was working! Matthew and William were surprised with the new style of playing of their opponents. In the end, Jack and Zack won the second set 7-5. Matthew and William were shocked! They thought they would win 6-0. If not 6-0, they thought they would surely win. Matthew and William were surprised that they lost, and even more so because they lost to the pair, whom they had just beaten 6-0 in the first set.

The winner of the third set would win the finals.

The third set oscillated between power and placement and was really entertaining. First, William or Mathew would hit a powerful shot, and Jack and Zack would go back and either chip the ball over the net or hit it in a corner. It was really fun, and in the end, the score from 0-0 ended up tied at 6-6.

The doubles finals would be decided by a tiebreaker!

The tiebreaker was so interesting that any person who was not carefully watching earlier also got up to see it. First, Matthew served, and Jack received and hit the ball in a corner from where William smacked the ball, and finally, Zack chipped the ball to make it 1-0. It went on and on and on till it was 13-13. Next serve, the ball fell in front of Jack, who hit it in the corner and got a point taking it to 14-13. Jack and Zack only needed one more point to win!

It was Jack's turn to serve for the championship point. He served, and Matthew picked it up well and then Zack delicately chipped the ball over Matthew. William dived to reach the ball, but just missed it!

Jack and Zack had won, and they were the youngest champions!

Jack and Zack fell on their knees. Bryan and Ryan jumped over the barricade and ran to Jack and Zack. Bryan and Ryan congratulated Jack and Zack, who then shook hands with the referee as well as their opponents – Matthew and William. Matthew told the winners, "You deserved to win." Jack replied, "You played well, and it deserved to be a tie. We actually won, luckily." William said, "Nonsense, you deserved to win, and you won a well-deserved one."

The coach was extremely happy for Jack and Zack, and warmly congratulated them.

The boys were called to receive the championship trophies, whose thin layer of gold, covering a metal base, was glittering. As the boys lifted the trophies, the whole crowd erupted with cheers. Zack told, "My brother and I dedicate this award to our tennis coach, Chris Wilson, and our two special friends."

Hearing this, the runners-up, William and Matthew, said, "You both are better

Jack and Zack won the tennis doubles trophies! They celebrated along with their friends - Bryan and Ryan - and their coach, Chris Wilson.

than my brother and me, and you are just eleven years old. Congratulations. You are nice guys giving credit to your coach and friends."

The coach was touched by Jack and Zack's words. Bryan and Ryan also got very emotional and embraced Jack and Zack. The quadruplets screamed as loud as they could.

Jack and Zack could not believe it. They never thought they would win after losing 6-0 in the first set. They were really thankful to their tennis coach for his strategy, which helped them win the final match.

Chapter - 4

The Trophies Whereabouts?

The boys – Jack, Zack, Bryan, and Ryan – went in the tennis coach's car to an inn called Coalsy Inn to enjoy the celebratory dinner and thereafter stay the night. All the winners of the tournament would stay the night at the Coalsy Inn after the finals, as the tournament finals were in London while teams were from neighbouring county of Kent.

The coach's car was a spacious one in which six people could fit in with ease. The trophies were safely kept on the front seat. There was place for four people on the back seat, and all the four boys squeezed together.

The four boys were really happy and were singing all the way to the inn. The song was created by the boys on the way, and they kept singing.

We are the Champions!

We are the Champions!

We won at the age of eleven.

We will not give up till we are thirty-seven.
We are the Champions!

We are the Champions!

We could not win without our guide.

Who helped us with all his might.
We are the Champions!

We are the Champions!

We could not do it without our friends.

Who helped us till the end of the tournaments.

We are the Champions!

We are the Champions!

The trophies which we are holding.

Are of gold and platinum and always shining.

We are the Champions!

We are the Champions!

The boys were exhausted but still very excited. They checked in at the Coalsy Inn. Jack and Zack went to their rooms, washed their faces and changed into evening wear.

Jack and Zack shared a room, while Bryan and Ryan shared another room, which was next to Jack and Zack's room.

Jack and Zack's room was a big one. It had two cupboards and two beds. There was a table where four people could sit. The beds were really soft and fluffy.

Bryan and Ryan's room was even more spacious. It had four cupboards and three beds. There was a small table next to the third bed. The beds were soft and fluffy as well.

Jack and Zack left their trophies on the table in their room. Then, they excitedly came down for dinner. At that same moment, they crashed into Bryan and Ryan, who were also coming for dinner. The boys could smell many kinds of food like stir-fried vegetables, bangers and mash, and toad in the hole. As they reached the table, they saw all the food, which looked delicious.

The coach welcomed them, and the four of them sat down and started feasting. First, the four boys started with fish and chips, and then, toad in the hole. They had some stir-fried vegetables along with bangers and mash. Just as they thought dinner was over, they were surprised to receive a cake in the shape of a trophy.

The cake was made of white chocolate for the metal part of the trophy and brown chocolate outside to show the gold covering of the trophy. The brown chocolate did not really look like gold, but the effect of the lights made it seem like gold. The trophy-shaped cake looked delightful. Bryan gave a slice of cake to the winners first. In half a minute, the first cake slice was devoured by Jack and Zack. The boys polished off the rest of the cake along with the coach. The boys were really exhausted, yet extremely happy. The four boys went to wash their hands and wished good night to the coach. The coach wanted to do some work and went to a different table towards a corner of the café. The four of them again sat at the same table and started to talk about the game.

Jack said, "Remember the time after the first set when we came to the coach and that time Bryan and Ryan just ran off. Zack and I thought that you both had abandoned us. But actually, you both had gone to get drums to cheer us." "And your faces were suddenly shocked when we started to play the drums. It was hilarious," said Bryan with a laugh. Zack said, "Yeah, we were shocked. But it gave us confidence." Bryan and Ryan boasted, "We tried to cheer you, and it worked. You won. Now, thank us if you don't mind, but even if you mind still thank us." Jack and Zack laughingly said, "OK, we'll thank you. Thank you, Bryan and Ryan. You fully deserve it." This amused all the four boys, and they all laughed. They talked for some more time, and just as they were about to go to their rooms, a waiter brought a glass of juice for each of them. The waiter told them it was a special juice sent by the coach to congratulate them. The boys happily started drinking the juice served by a young and smiling waiter.

The boys liked the waiter and started asking about him. His name was Nicolas Allen, and he was an eighteen-year-old boy with an olive complexion and jet-black hair. His height was five feet six inches. He had a habit of winking, which made him easily recognisable. Nicholas became their friend and was called Nico by his new friends. Nico had grown up in a foster home with his brother and did not know anything about his parents. Since his childhood he had assumed his parents were not alive. Nico and his brother had to earn money themselves. Nico was working in Coalsy Inn and earning a low salary. Somehow, he was managing to live in this small amount.

The four boys got instant energy after drinking the juice and thus wanted to play. They had nothing to play, so they decided to play 'Guess the Number'. Jack did not know how to play, so first, there was a demonstration for Jack. Then, the game commenced, and

Bryan chose the first number without telling Zack. First, Zack guessed '54'. Bryan said, "More." Ryan guessed '61'. "More," Bryan said, and then Jack said '77'. Bryan said, "Less." Finally, Zack got it right by guessing '73'. They played for some more time, and then when Bryan glanced at his watch, he was surprised to see it was almost 10:00 p.m.

The waiter, Nico, offered to get a cup of cappuccino to the coach. The tennis coach looked tired and sleepy. After every tournament, the tennis coach would write about the tournament. He gladly drank the cappuccino and then continued writing. When he saw the boys, he smiled and asked if everything was alright. The boys said, "Everything is fine, coach."

The boys felt really happy for the wonderful day, followed by a great evening and went back to their rooms. Bryan and Ryan were about to start changing when they heard a cry coming from Jack and Zack's room. Bryan and Ryan hastened to Jack and Zack's room and, when they opened the door, they saw Zack crying while Jack was trying to console his brother.

Jack and Zack sadly informed the shocking development to Bryan and Ryan. When Jack and Zack had entered the room after dinner, they did not see the trophies on the table. Zack had kept both the trophies on the table before he went down to have dinner.

Bryan said forcefully, "Now, let's search the whole room. The trophies would be here somewhere." The boys searched the room, but to their shock, they could not find the trophies. Finally, they went outside the room and started to search the inn. When they reached down, they met the tennis coach and the waiter Nico, who was serving drinks to the guests. They told both of them about the loss of the trophies. The coach was also shocked, and so was their new friend, Nico. All of them started to search for the trophies. They searched everywhere in the inn, but they could not find the trophies. All of them searched once again, but the search was in vain.

The boys were shocked to see the empty table and realised that the trophies were missing.

They sat sadly in the inn's café and thought what could have happened to the trophies. They concluded that someone might have stolen them while they were having dinner. All of them felt disheartened and sadly returned to their rooms, where they could not sleep, as they were thinking about the trophies.

Finally, after some time, Bryan and Ryan decided to go to Jack and Zack's room. Jack and Zack were awake but surprised to see the two of them. Before they could say anything, Ryan told, "Don't worry and go to sleep. We will do something together. We cannot lose your trophies." Then he closed the door. Thereafter, both of them went back to their room and fell asleep. The four of them were finally asleep well past midnight.

The next morning, they checked the inn again for the trophies. But still no news.

Finally, in the late afternoon, the boys, along with their coach, sadly left the Coalsy Inn to go back to their school. The friendly waiter, Nico, especially came to see them off and gave a warm hug to each one of them along with his trademark wink.

Chapter - 5

Any Lead to Find the Trophies?

The boys were sitting at the breakfast table back in their school, still thinking about how to get the trophies back. The trophies that they had won and also shockingly lost two days back.

It was important to get the trophies back soon to be in time for the mayor's event, where Jack and Zack would be presented with the trophies by the mayor himself. The boys did not know what to do next. They had no leads.

The whole day passed, and the boys somehow managed to spend the day thinking about what to do next.

The next morning, the boys again met for breakfast. Jack and Zack had started to give up on finding the trophies and looked very glum. Bryan and Ryan said that they would get breakfast for the winners. They wanted to do something to cheer Jack and Zack.

While Bryan and Ryan were going to get breakfast for the four of them, they had a glance on the newspaper stand and saw a local county newspaper. The headline of the local county newspaper said, *"Tennis Winners' Trophies Stolen Yesterday."*

Bryan and Ryan rushed to Jack and Zack with the newspaper and read the article on the trophies being stolen. The article said:

Tennis Winners' Trophies Stolen Yesterday

After Arthur Wright and Colin Johnson won the tennis doubles tournament in Woodland Park stadium in London, misfortune came tumbling down their way. Their trophies were stolen in Coalsy Inn. The boys went to have dinner and when they came back to their room, the trophies were not there. They were gone. The boys are from the city of Ashford in the county of Kent.

The boys were shocked. Same tournament, at the same location and trophies are stolen from the same inn. Finally, there was a lead for the boys. After reading the article, the boys were determined that they had to get their and others' trophies back.

The boys decided that they should take help from an elder and decided to go to their tennis coach, Chris Wilson.

The four of them told the coach about the loss of the trophies of other winners also. The boys told him, "We think there is a pattern. In every tournament, when the winners go to the Coalsy Inn to spend the night, the thieves strike. Our guess is that when the winners go for dinner, the thieves come into the room and take the trophies, just like what happened to us the other night. Coach, can you please tell us when is the next final of the tournament? We can go there along with you and possibly find out who has stolen our trophies. We worked so hard, and now we don't have the trophies. It's like all our efforts were in vain. We have to get them back. Please help us coach."

The tennis coach said, "The tournament's next final is tomorrow at the same venue in London, and I need to plan if I have to take you there tomorrow."

The boys were very happy, as they thought they finally had some lead to get back their trophies. The coach suggested that the boys do something to relax.

The boys seemed happy with some hope, and decided to play a game of chess. Jack said with a laugh, "The game is between me and Bryan, and Zack vs Ryan. It's like semi-finals, and winners play finals." Bryan had a style of recklessly killing his opponent's pieces but also getting his pieces killed. This strategy sometimes worked, but not always. Jack used to play by killing his opponent's pieces, not recklessly like Bryan, but slowly and strategically. This was a more efficient method than Bryan's, and that's why others thought Jack would win.

The first game of chess was a really entertaining one. It was not one-sided, but was a balanced game with both players playing well. Each of the players had their own strategy, which was always broken down by reckless killing of the opponent's chess pieces while being driven by the overall strategy to win. The winner of the chess game was Jack, who checkmated Bryan just a move before Bryan could checkmate him. Bryan was not a sore loser, having lost so narrowly, though he was sad because he lost. Jack was happy he could finally win the chess game and a chance to win something. Bryan had told before the game, "The winner will get something."

The second chess game's contestants were Zack and Ryan. Ryan was not very good at the game, but still, beginners could win. Zack was a defensive player, but whenever he had the opportunity to strike and checkmate, he would always do it and never miss a chance to win. The game started and the game was pretty much one-sided. Ryan was attacking his best, and Zack was defending. Still, Zack's defensive pieces would kill Ryan's pieces. In the end, surprisingly Zack won. Zack killed many pieces of the opponent till only the king and a few pawns were left with the opponent, and then, in a couple of moves the game was over.

Twin brothers, Jack and Zack, were supposed to play the chess finals. Sibling rivalry is well known, and this was a really big fight on the chessboard, with each side having a king and battling with their respective queen, rooks, bishops, knights and pawns. Finally, one brother would become victorious.

The game was attacking strategy vs defensive strategy. The game started well. Jack, with his attacking style, was unable to get his strategy to work as Zack was too defensive. Jack tried his best but after some time he accidentally left an empty gap, so Zack could attack from there and finally was able to checkmate Jack instantly.

Zack was happy he won. He was eagerly waiting for his winning gift, which he knew Bryan would give him. He got a *Hot Wheels* Racer Car, which he really liked. The car was long, and it went from broad in the front to narrow at the rear. The best part was that it had a logo of two tennis rackets; the handle of the rackets overlapped on the narrowest part, while the broadest part of the car had two seats where people could sit. The seating area of the car was white, and the remaining was blue. Zack was really happy when he got the chess winner's prize, and he knew he could not have done it without concentration and focus. So, he said to himself, "If one is concentrated and focused, he gets rewards like winning a game or maybe even something more special."

After eating lunch, the four boys decided to laze around and just read a book each. Then, the boys decided to have an afternoon nap. The boys slept for some time. When they woke up, they were surprised as it was only 5:00 p.m.; the boys didn't expect to sleep for just an hour. They thought that they would sleep till 6:00 p.m. at least. They lay on the bed but could not sleep anymore, and finally they decided to get up. Even though they did not sleep, they rested themselves for the day.

The boys went to the hall and talked about their plans for the next day. They concluded that the boys would book a room at the same Coalsy Inn and act like normal guests. They would book a room close to the winners' room and keep a watch for the thieves when they enter the winners' room to steal the trophies. Thereafter, the four of them would follow the thieves to where all the other trophies were kept, and then they would ensure that all the trophies are distributed to the rightful winners. Subsequently, Jack and Zack would hand over their trophies to the mayor, and then the mayor would honour the winners with the trophies at the important event. The plan seemed pretty simple.

The boys planned to have a quick dinner, but it got prolonged as they were talking about their next steps. Ryan said excitedly, "Right. There is no way our plan can go wrong." "Yes, you're right," replied Jack jokingly. Jack added, "Don't you get it? The location of the inn is slightly towards the right of the city, so you're right." All of them laughed.

Then the boys went outside to the ground to get some fresh air and also to think about a few more plans, just in case they could get an even better plan. They were thinking that after working out a few plans, they would compare all their plans and then decide which one would be the most efficient one and use that plan for the next day. The boys thought of not a few but many plans.

The boys' new plans were also good, but not as good as the first one, so the four of them decided to stick with their original plan only. The boys decided to eat dinner at 6:15 p.m. and then go to sleep. The boys wanted to have a small and quick dinner, and they succeeded in doing so. The boys brushed and changed into their night suits, and they were off to bed. The boys tried to sleep but could not sleep immediately. It took about half an hour for Zack to fall asleep followed by Bryan. Five minutes later, both Jack and Ryan were also fast asleep along with Zack and Bryan.

The next morning, the boys got up fresh and excited about the day. The quadruplets knew that the tennis tournament winners would reach Coalsy Inn somewhere late evening or early night, but the boys decided to go in the morning itself so that they could book their room at the inn in advance and then be ready at their positions. The boys weren't in a hurry, and they ate a nice, slow and relaxed breakfast that was extended from their usual time of around fifteen minutes to half an hour. The boys also knew the drive to Coalsy Inn from their school was around two hours, so they decided to eat a heavier breakfast than usual. They also packed the remaining sandwiches and planned to eat them on their way to Coalsy Inn.

Each of the boys had different things for breakfast. Ryan had bread and bacon, Bryan had a ham sandwich, Jack a sausage sandwich, and Zack had scrambled eggs. After eating their hearty breakfast, the boys changed their clothes and started to look for their tennis coach. The boys searched everywhere, and finally, they found him waiting for them next to his car. The boys were happy to see the coach and jumped into the back seat of the car.

The boys were thrilled and enjoyed their ride to Coalsy Inn. The scenery was beautiful and relaxing. After an hour in the car, the boys decided to have their remaining share of the sandwiches. The boys finished their share in less than a minute and then they decided that they would again go through their plan and see if it would work.

They continued discussing their plan until they reached the town and then they went into the Coalsy Inn. There, they saw the receptionist and were lucky as no one was near him. The boys ran towards the receptionist. A man was approaching the receptionist, but Bryan recklessly slid in front of the man so that the four of them could come before him in the line. The man did not see Bryan on the floor in front of him and fell over him. Watching this, the boys laughed at the man's unawareness. The man got up and looked angrily towards the boys. The boys had a glance at his face. His face looked cruel! He had a mutton chop beard.

Bryan quickly asked the receptionist, "Which room are the winners going to come in?" The receptionist said, "They will come in room number 5." The boys knew that room number 6 was next to 5. As they had seen in the inn's map, on the first floor, if one went straight, one would see rooms 1 and 2. On the right were rooms 3 and 4. On the left there were rooms 5 and 6. While rooms 7 and 8 were next to rooms 1 and 2, rooms 9 and 10 were located next to rooms 3 and 4. On the ground floor, there was a café where food was served. The café was a large dining hall. On the left side of the café was a washroom. Exactly opposite the washroom was the kitchen. The boys had understood all the key locations of the inn. The boys were very keen to move in to room number 6, next to the winners' room number 5.

The boys asked for room number 6, and the receptionist agreed and handed over the keys to them. The man, whom Bryan had moved ahead of in the line, also wanted the same room. He complained, pointing to Bryan, "This boy tripped me and stole my room. Send him and his friends out of the hotel and also forbid them to come again."

The boys were shocked by the man's behaviour, but anyway they quickly went to room number 6 before anything else could happen. Room 6 was huge. It had four beds, two tables with six chairs and four separate cupboards. The boys wanted to drink water, as they were thirsty. So, they left their bags in the room. Bryan left his bag on the first bed, Ryan on the second, Zack on the third and Jack on the fourth.

The boys went to the café and saw a glimpse of their friendly waiter, Nicolas, whom they used to call Nico. The five of them were like good friends when they met last time. Nico also saw them, but surprisingly quickly turned his face away when the boys looked at him. Before the boys could even call him, Nico hastened inside the kitchen. The boys sat at a table waiting for a waiter when suddenly, from the kitchen, Nico came out with four glasses of fresh orange juice. He suddenly approached the boys smiling and winking, and then said, "Orange juice for you four. This is like a welcome drink from my side."

Then the boys also smiled and decided to tell Nico why they had come. Jack started excitedly, "Remember we came just a few days back." Nico nodded. Bryan continued, "That night only, our trophies were stolen! You remember the trophies were stolen while we were eating dinner. So, we think, the thieves will again steal the trophies tonight, when the winners of the today's finals come to the inn. We are going to see and hear if anything is suspicious." "If anything," said Ryan with a serious face.

The boys went to their coach, Chris Wilson, and asked him if they could play in the garden of the inn. The coach laughed and said, "You are old enough to be anywhere inside the boundary wall of the inn. There's no need to ask me."

The boys went to play football. Bryan and Ryan were good football players, just like Jack and Zack were good tennis players. In the excitement, the boys made the mistake of leaving the ball in their room. The boys then quickly went back and got the football. The game was between Bryan and Zack versus Ryan and Jack. They decided to have one twin in one team to balance both teams. The game was dominated by Bryan and Ryan, though playing in different teams, as they had gone through rigorous football training.

The quality of the game was a pleasure for the eye. First, the score went 1-0 to Bryan and Zack's team, when Bryan played a simple pass to Zack, who passed him back and set Bryan up for a goal with a simple tap-in. The scores were equal when Ryan scored a long ranger into the goal. The game went on and on from 0-0 to 1-1 to 11-11. After Jack equalised to make the score 11-11, Bryan had a glance at his watch and decided to do a penalty shoot-out to decide the winner of the football match.

First, the boys had to decide which team would shoot first in the penalty shoot-out. Instead of a toss, Bryan came up with an interesting idea. He said to the other team, "Jack and Ryan. If you can guess which hour it is, you can choose whether to start the penalty shoot-out." Bryan had specially asked the question at that time so as to confuse Jack and Ryan between 5:59 and 6:00 p.m. Bryan further added, "You will have to answer before I count to three. OK I will start now. One, Two." Jack interrupted, "It's 5 o'clock something now, not 6 o'clock as yet." The exact time was 5:59:59 p.m. – just a second before 6:00 p.m. Jack was correct, and his team decided to shoot first.

First, Jack took the shot and slotted it inside the goal. Next was Zack from the other team, who hit the shot in the corner accurately. Like this, it went on to 4-4. It was Bryan's turn to take his team's final penalty kick, but he missed! It was time for Ryan to bring it home by putting the ball into the goal. The shot was well placed and in the corner of the goal, but it was stopped by Zack! So, it was a draw!

Jack stole a quick glance at Bryan's watch and told the rest of the boys that they had to go back. The boys went to find their friend Nico, and when they found him, they asked him for four glasses of orange juice. He agreed and got it in less than two minutes. The boys happily drank the juice and went to their rooms.

The boys were waiting for the winners to enter their room, and the winners finally came happily, holding their trophies with them.

After they changed, the winners opened the door of their room and went down to the café to have dinner. At that time, the quadruplets opened their room's door and decided to pretend to play a game of chess on the table from where they could see if anyone was entering the room of the winners. The boys waited and waited, but nobody entered the winners' room. They decided that they would talk about the football game to pass the time while looking at the winners' room. The boys kept talking about their football match while waiting. Jack said, "Remember my penalty. It was going to go in the bottom corner, but it hit the pole. I was so unlucky." "And I was even more," said Ryan.

The boys suddenly saw a movement outside and went to see the person more clearly, but to their dismay, it was not the thief but the winners coming back into their room. The quadruplets concluded that the day's winners did not lose their trophies.

Suddenly, the boys heard a loud cry from the winners' room. The latest winners had lost their trophies too. The quadruplets, who were kind at heart, immediately went to the winners' room to console them. The winners were comforted by each of the quadruplets – Jack, Zack, Bryan, and Ryan. The four of them promised the winners, who had also lost the trophies, that they would get their trophies back.

All the four boys were shocked and were thinking how could the trophies be stolen without anybody going through the door of the room. After lots and lots of thinking but without answers, the boys fell asleep, dreaming of finding the trophies.

Chapter - 6

Promising Leads

The boys woke up the next morning feeling dejected. They had no more ideas on how to get the trophies back. They wanted to stop solving the mystery of the missing trophies and wanted to leave the inn.

When they went down for breakfast, they were surprised as their friend and waiter Nico wasn't there. They ordered their breakfast and sadly sat down to eat. They saw Nico but as they were feeling gloomy, they did not talk to him. It looked like he was searching for someone, but he was not able to find him or her.

The boys started eating their breakfast, and then they noticed that Nico had found the person he was looking for. After the boys finished eating breakfast, suddenly Nico came.

Nico was panting and quickly told, "He said to safely hide the trophies once the job is over." Bryan asked, "Who?" "The manager," Nico answered.

Ryan said, "Catch your breath, and delineate the information slowly."

Nico caught his breath and said, "The manager asked me to get him a cup of tea late last night. When I reached the door, I heard the manager saying to some person to safely hide the trophies once the job is over. I wanted to tell you this important information. I decided to tell you after you all had finished your breakfast and when nobody was around you."

Ryan asked, "Who is this manager?"

Nico explained, "The manager's name is Mr. Graham Boggs. He manages the inn. Nobody likes him in this inn, as he is considered a bad man. He is known to have issues with money. Mr Boggs keeps borrowing money from many people for personal reasons."

Bryan enthusiastically said, "We have finally got some lead."

Listening to this new information, the four of them decided to continue staying in the inn.

Jack had an idea and said to the others, "Maybe Mr. Boggs knows who is stealing it. Or even worse, could he be the thief? That is why we need to spy on him, and we have just the person who should do it. Nico shall do it. He is a waiter at this inn, and nobody will doubt him. He shall make it look like he is a kind-hearted person and will frequently ask the manager if he wants anything. But before going into the manager's room, he shall hear if the manager is saying something."

Jack added further, after thinking for some time, "We will order something every hour at this café. Nico, you will act like our team member. When the person at the café prepares our bill for our food, Nico, you will go and say that you are only seeing if the money mentioned on the bill is correct or not.

In this way, Nico, you send us any message through our bill. You can write the message and your name on the back side of our bill." After a deep breath, Jack further added, "This is only to make sure Nico is not meeting us or making gestures to us. This is to be done just so that nobody gets to know Nico is part of our team and what we are doing."

Bryan was astounded by Jack's thinking and complimented, "What a brainwave."

While everyone was giving compliments to Jack, Zack was in a mind of his own. Zack said, "What if the manager, Mr Boggs, or his assistants get to know about Nico's plans of giving a message on the back of the bill. In such a case, Nico will be in trouble because of us. Maybe we should give all of us code names. We never know if any of us has to give some important and urgent message to the other person, so code names are a good idea. People will just think it as some blabbering by someone."

Zack decided to tell the rest, "Guys, we need code names. If the manager or some of his assistants see the message, Nico will get in trouble because of us. And if we can't speak to each other, we may have to give an important message. That is why we need code names."

The rest agreed and they all said together, "Let's make code names." Jack decided to keep his code name simple. It was his full name's initial, *JP,* which stood for Jack Pietersen. Zack decided to interchange the first and second alphabets, third and fourth, and so on of his first name and surname. His code was *azkc iptereesn*. Nico decided to give a simple one as his code name. It was the opposite of the name of the 'Coalsy' inn. It was *yslaoc*. Bryan's code name was something which no one would expect. It was the word 'code name' spelled backwards. His code name was *eman edoc*. Ryan decided that he would only change the letters of his first name. His code was the second simplest. It was *yarn*. It was a small word, but no one would suspect it was Ryan.

They decided to order something every hour to enable Nico to pass on any message to them. Nico was about to come near them, when Ryan warned him not to come near them to raise any suspicion.

The boys decided to go to their rooms and know more about sports through reading books. They had to spend time somehow. Bryan and Ryan read about football, as they played football, while Jack and Zack read about tennis, as they played tennis.

The football book was about skill moves and how to perfect them. The tennis book was about how to improve one's tennis serve and how to hit the ball more accurately. The boys were busy reading when Bryan remembered that they had read for a little more than one hour, and it was time to get something from the café and to see if Nico had any message for them. He had to do the big job of getting the rest of them to come down to earth by stopping them to read. The job was very difficult, as all were too busy reading. Somehow with a little bit of pushing, he finally achieved it. At that moment, they had to hurry to the café to get something so that if Nico had a message, they could receive it. They just ordered a croissant for each of them and asked for the bill with the croissant.

When the bill came with the croissant the boys flipped the bill, but to their utter disappointment, there was nothing. The boys enjoyed their croissant, and when they finished eating, it was around 11:00 a.m. Hence, the boys decided to again go back to their room. Each of them again started reading his book, from where each boy had stopped, and finished reading it. By the time they finished reading the books, it was time for lunch.

The boys went to have their lunch, but first they only ordered an orange juice each to see if Nico had a message for them or not. The juice didn't come for a long time, but then finally, it came along with the bill after seventeen minutes of ordering. Bryan took the bill, flipped it around, and said with a sigh, "No message."

The boys ordered juicy chicken steaks with mashed potatoes. The boys relished their lunch and were satisfied. But there was still no message.

The boys went to their room to get their football, and then they went out to play football. To learn their codes, they made the teams in their new code names. The teams were *JP* and *azkc iptereesn* vs *eman edoc* and *yarn*. All four of them thought *eman edoc* and *yarn* would win as they played football and were more experienced. *JP* and *azkc iptereesn* were always underrated in the game, as they were tennis players.

The game started and was dominated by Bryan and Ryan, and within the first few minutes, they had scored two goals. Jack and Zack were good at attacking, but bad at defending, yet they still managed to score three goals. Unluckily, they conceded three goals as well. The scores went till 7-6 to Bryan and Ryan. Bryan was about to blow the final whistle just when suddenly Jack shot from pretty far out. The ball flew all the way into the opponent's goal. The ball went in the goal just before Bryan blew the whistle. Bryan and Ryan were adamant in saying it was not a goal, but in their hearts, they knew it was a goal. Ryan felt unhappy lying, so told the truth that it should be given a goal, and the score became 7-7.

The four boys decided to go back to the dining hall to see if Nico had a message for them or not. The four boys got four lemonades and four jam sandwiches, and then asked for the bill with the food. This time, the boys were sure that Nico had a message for them. The boys were so sure that they decided to eat their snack first. Before reading the message from Nico, the boys enjoyed the sandwich. The sandwich was delicious and the four boys, after eating, decided to see the message. Bryan flipped the bill around and to their disappointment there was nothing.

The boys knew that the next meal they would eat was dinner, so the boys went out to play football. The boys continued playing the same football match and the score was levelled at 15-15. Jack decided that they should do a penalty shoot-out to decide the winner.

First, Bryan took the penalty. He coolly did a 'Panenka' shot, and it worked. Jack decided that he would hit on the left side of the keeper but in the last second, he decided to hit it on the right side of the keeper. This made his shot go wide and outside the goal. The score was 1-0 to Bryan and Ryan. Ryan hit the ball in the right top corner. The keeper had no idea where the shot was going and couldn't stop it. Zack was up next, and he knew he could not miss. He decided to smack the ball with all his power in the middle. Luckily, the shot was not very powerful; if it were then the ball would have gone over the bar and not into the goal. Bryan hit the ball in the left bottom corner, and it went in. Jack smacked the ball, but it went too high. The shot was skied and missed the goal. It was all up to Ryan.

Ryan decided to do a trick shot. It was the stutter step. He ran fast and then in the last second slowed for a second and saw the goalkeeper Jack diving to the left. This made

Ryan's decision very easy. He just passed the ball slowly towards the other side of the goal. The ball was rolling into the net. Jack, who had dived to the other side, got up and tried to stop it by diving to the side of the ball and somehow managed to stop the ball from going in. The score was 3-1. Zack calmly curled the ball in the top right corner and made it 3-2.

Bryan felt pity for his brother, who had missed the last shot, and he asked him to take this penalty and win it for them by scoring. Ryan decided to end the game in style by doing a Panenka. The goalkeeper, Jack, was cautious and decided to dive after he had a glance at where the ball was going. As he saw the ball coming in the middle, he decided to stay and when the ball came, he pushed it away. Finally, it was all up to Jack if he scored the goal, then the game would go to sudden death penalty shoot-out. But if he missed, they would lose. Jack decided to keep it simple. Blast the ball in the right top corner. He executed his part perfectly, but Bryan jumped like an acrobat and pushed the ball out.

Compliments came from everywhere, "Bryan, you are the best keeper." Others added, "You are better than Iker Casillas. Even world-famous goal keepers Manuel Neuer and Gianluigi Buffon are nowhere near you."

The four boys felt that Nico might not have a message for them. They ordered their dinner and hoped for the best. The boys got four plates of pasta loaded with vegetables and white sauce. The pasta looked delightful and tasted even better. The creamy white sauce just melted in their mouths and the pasta was so soft. The boys loved the meal and, when they got the bill, there was no information, just like they had guessed. The boys were too tired to even say goodnight. They went to bed and dozed off almost immediately.

The boys were sleeping when Ryan heard a person running across the corridors. He decided not to wake up the rest, as it was early in the morning and decided to follow the person all alone. He quietly opened the door of his room and closed it softly. Thereafter, Ryan slowly walked towards the place from where he was still hearing the footsteps.

He saw a man turning open the door of the manager's room, and Ryan waited until the man went inside the room. Thereafter, Ryan ran towards the room and stood next to it. The door of the room was not fully closed. Ryan heard the manager, Mr. Boggs, saying, "You, have the window opening instrument?" "Yes, obviously," came another voice, which seemed like a known voice. "Ok you can go now," Mr. Boggs said. Ryan hid on the side until the man came out. He saw the same man, who had asked the receptionist to forbid them from entering the inn; the same man who also wanted their room in the inn.

Ryan decided to go back to the room and tell the rest. He went to the room and was surprised, as he did not find anyone in the room. He decided to tell the other three later, as he thought they would be eating breakfast. At that moment, he had to tell Nico. Nico could help in getting more information on this. Just then he heard the manager loudly calling Nico and telling him, "Come to my room. I have lots of work for you." Ryan expected Nico would soon be entering Mr. Boggs' room. Ryan wanted to inform Nico to meet him to tell the latest news.

Ryan had to somehow send a coded message to Nico to meet him somewhere else so that Mr. Boggs does not know about it. Also, he wanted Nico to see the message before he entered the manager's room. Suddenly, an idea stuck Ryan. Ryan went to the kitchen, got paper, and used the glue stick, which he saw lying in the corridor.

Ryan stuck pieces of paper from just outside the manager's door to a corner of the corridor. On the pieces of paper, he made arrows pointing to the side towards the next paper and so on. The series of papers with arrows were from the manager's room to a corner of the corridor. On the last paper at the end of the corridor, Ryan mentioned *'flip by yarn'*.

Nico was about to enter into the manager's room, when he saw the arrow marks on the paper. First, he ignored it, and later thought could be a code from the boys. He followed it until he reached the last paper that mentioned '*flip by yarn*'. He thought, "This is some code."

At first Nico did not understand it. Then he thought again. Nico remembered '*yarn*' was code for Ryan. The word '*flip*' meant flip the paper. He flipped the paper, and it was mentioned on the back side '*win the last three of meadow*'. He knew it couldn't be too obvious. It had to be coded. He thought, "What is the last three of *meadow*. The last three of what? Is there a meadow anywhere here?" He thought again, "Maybe it the last three letters of meadow. Yes, '*dow*' and '*win*'." Nico further thought, "What could it mean? '*Dowwin*' No. '*Window*' yeah." Nico understood what Ryan was trying to tell him. There seemed to be some connection with the windows. Nico concluded in his mind, "Ryan has sent a message of something to do with windows. Does it mean that the stolen trophies have some connection with the windows?"

Meanwhile Ryan had gone to the hall to accompany his mates and tell them the story. When Ryan reached, he saw Nico serving breakfast to the boys. Seeing Ryan, Nico told him, "Got your message. Can you tell more about it?" Ryan asked Nico to stay for some time and listen, even though it was risky as Nico could get caught. All four of them had a story to tell.

First was Jack who told his story. He started, "Yesterday late night I went for a walk outside. At that time, I saw someone carrying an instrument-like thing. I didn't tell you then because I was too sleepy."

Next was Bryan. He said, "Yesterday night, I couldn't sleep, so I went outside to calm my nerves with nature. I was admiring it when I saw a person looking intently at the window of a room from outside. This is the same room that the winners stay in. I couldn't tell you because you were asleep."

Next, it was Zack's turn. He started off, "I slept early last night, so I woke up in the morning and saw that Ryan was not there. I went to the washroom, did my daily routine, and then went out for a walk. While passing through the corridor, I overheard outside the manager's room, 'We need this instrument today'."

Ryan told, "My story is the answer to yours. While all of you were asleep, I heard the sounds of someone running. So, without waking anyone of you, I went out and followed that man. The same man who wanted our room. The manager, Mr. Boggs, asked him if he had that the instrument. I think this is the same instrument you three saw or heard."

Ryan concluded, "There is some connection between the instrument-like thing, the winners' window from outside, and the trophies."

Ryan further added, "So, we understand it now. I guess we should stay outside to catch the thieves." Came Bryan's voice, "No, all of us should not." Jack finally suggested, "Two of us should stay in the same place like last time, inside the inn. While the other two should stay outside. We never know what is really happening." "Yeah, that's a good point," the rest agreed. The boys were happy and when they had their breakfast, they were still talking about their latest discovery.

After listening, Nico quietly went back to the kitchen hoping that no one had seen him.

Most importantly, the boys knew they finally had some serious leads.

Chapter - 7

The Thieves Strike Again

The boys went to their room, after finishing their breakfast. Ryan said excitedly, "We now have a real chance to catch the thieves. We have to do our best today evening, when the thieves strike again to steal today's doubles winners' trophies."

Bryan added happily, "Yes. We will catch the thieves today and get the trophies back to our dearest friends, Jack and Zack, and also to other winners." Ryan jumped up and said, "Let's go and see the famous Hyde Park in London. We have never visited this majestic park. It's not too far from this inn. Let's enjoy during the day and then catch the thieves in the evening."

The boys decided to go to the famous Hyde Park to celebrate. The inn was not very far from Hyde Park in London. The boys told all the latest developments to the coach and also took his permission to go to the park. The coach said, "I will drop you there and pick you up on the way back. I also have some work today at the tennis association's office that is near Hyde Park. Enjoy your day." The boys were really excited.

The boys were surprised to see the beauty of Hyde Park. The trees in Hyde Park were of many varieties; some of them were huge with wide trunks. The four boys walked to the Apsley Gate. There were so many people, and the sight of the gate was so inviting. It was one of the most beautiful things the four boys had seen. Next, the boys went to the Queen Elizabeth Gate, which was even more beautiful than the Aspley Gate, and the boys loved it. Thereafter, the boys went to the Achilles Statue. It was eighteen feet high and was made to commemorate the life of Arthur Wellesley. He was the Duke of Wellington and the victor of the Battle of Waterloo. It was the first statue installed in Hyde Park. After that, the boys went to the café near Serpentine Lake and ate a croissant each. Then, the boys walked along the Serpentine Lake, admiring its beauty, and talking about the history of the park.

The boys kept track of time and were ready to be picked up by the coach. They returned back to the inn more than an hour before the winners of the tennis tournament were expected to come to the inn.

In the meantime, at the inn, the boys ate a fulfilling meal of fish and chips with mashed potatoes. The potatoes had a nice taste that melted in the mouth. The fish was very soft and tender. The boys loved it and slowly enjoyed their meal. It was one of the most delicious foods they had ever eaten. The four of them were impressed as they never thought such delicious food could be made at inns. The boys got their bill; just like earlier they weren't expecting anything from friendly waiter Nico. Just as they guessed, there was nothing written.

The four boys, after eating, decided that they would help the staff by doing errands at the inn. The boys' plan was to somehow roam inside the inn and maybe get some clues. They went to Nico and asked him, "Hey Nico, do you have anything that needs to be done at the inn for you?" Nico replied, "I don't have any errands which you can do, but you can go to Big Billy. He never finishes anything on time. You four know Big Billy, don't you?" The four didn't even know that someone had Big Billy as his name. Jack sarcastically asked, "Is he that bulky man who's always complaining?" Nico said, "No, the tall, lean man who's always with a stick, and he sounds like a pirate. At least, that's what I think. He usually is in the room where all the things like blankets, sheets for beds and other housekeeping articles are kept." The boys understood that Nico was helping them and thanked him.

The boys were excited and went to Big Billy. The boys entered into the room, that Nico had explained, and they heard a person say, "Argh, mate. Why are you here?" "So, that's

Big Billy," the four boys whispered. Bryan said, "We're here to help you." "Good, you have come. I have loads to do. I would really appreciate it if you could take these sheets and put them on all the beds of the ten rooms in the inn," said Big Billy smilingly.

The boys counted the sheets and found out there were sixteen. Bryan, whose brain worked really fast, said, "One sheet in seven rooms, four sheets in one room, three sheets in one room and two in one." The rest said, "Wow! That was fast." Bryan politely accepted the praise from his friends. The boys were excited, as this gave them a chance to visit all the rooms of the inn. Just in case it could lead him them to some clue.

The boys decided that each one of them would carry four sheets. The boys made different sets of sheets as per the number of beds in the rooms. Seven sets of one sheet each, a set of four sheets, one set of three sheets and the last set of two sheets. The plan was that inside each room, two boys would open a folded sheet and give it to the other two boys, who would take the sheet and put it on the bed and so on. The boys worked smartly and quickly finished their job and went back to Big Billy. Big Billy said, "Finished?" "Yes," the boys replied. "You can go and do what you want," said Big Billy. Thereafter, the boys went to Nico to ask him if there were any more clues for them.

Suddenly, they saw two stylish boys coming inside the inn. At first, they forgot who those two were, but then suddenly remembered they would be the winners of that day's tennis tournament. All the four boys quickly went to their positions. Bryan and Ryan stood outside their room, while Jack and Zack took their place outside the inn. The four boys were ready at their agreed places.

It looked like the two winners were changing into more stylish clothes because they were taking a long time inside their room. Finally, the winners opened the door of their room, and they came out. Surprisingly, they immediately went back inside their room.

Again, the winners took time. This time, they did not take as long as last time. Bryan said, "Even the thieves would be bored to death waiting for these winners."

Both the winners finally came out after an hour, and they indeed looked very cool. The winners walked smartly and went down to the main hall of the inn to celebrate their win. The quadruplets were ready with their plan to look out for the trophy thieves. For a long time, no one came, and the quadruplets thought no one would come and the winners of that day's tournament would have their trophies safely with them. Jack and Zack were waiting outside the inn, and they were almost asleep. Zack's eyelids were drooping, and he was yawning like crazy.

The boys were suddenly awakened when they saw two men outside the window of the winners' room holding something that looked like a modified pair of scissors. The boys thought, "Can this be what Ryan had overheard about and could it be used to open the window?"

The boys saw the way the two men meticulously opened the window from outside. They used an instrument which was like a pair of scissors, but slightly different. When the top part of the instrument was closed, it was so thin that it could fit through the small gap between the two sashes of the closed window. The thieves first inserted the top part of the instrument in between the two sashes of the closed window. Thereafter, they opened the instrument to stretch it out and move upwards, where there was a bolt inside the window. This bolt was holding the two sashes thus locking the window. The interesting point was that, with a slight pressure, this instrument would then force the bolt open. In this way, they could open the window of the room from outside.

As per plan, Jack and Zack did not stop the thieves from opening the window from outside, as they wanted to make sure they were the trophy thieves.

It was a really beautiful way of opening the window from outside. Even Jack and Zack were admiring it even though they knew they should not because their own trophies were also stolen by them in a similar fashion. Jack and Zack were unable to see the thieves' faces. The only thing that caught their eye was that the thieves wore gloves and socks to not let anybody get their footprint or handprint.

Meanwhile, another development was taking place inside the inn. Bryan and Ryan were inside the inn and could hear some noise inside the winners' room and wanted to check. They went down in search of Nico because he'd know where the key to the room was. The boys searched for Nico but could not find him. They finally saw him serving tea to a man dressed in a black suit with a white shirt and a tie, and black pants with matching belt and shoes. He seemed like an old man, as he had white hair and a white moustache. While Nico was going to the kitchen after serving, they went up to him and asked, "Hey, can you give us the key to the winners' room, please? We think the thieves are there. We are hearing many sounds from inside the room while the winners are eating dinner down in the hall." Nico replied, "I can't give it to you, but I'll go to the winners' room and open it for you."

The boys accompanied Nico as he went to the receptionist, Mr. Noah Atkinson. Mr. Noah Atkinson had a neat desk. He was wearing a white shirt with a black and blue striped tie, a grey coat, grey pants with a black belt, and white shoes. He had a moustache, was bald and bespectacled, and was a nice person.

Mr. Atkinson was sitting on a blue chair, ready to help anyone and everyone. Nico asked him, "Can you please give me the key to room number 5 please." Mr. Atkinson was a good man, but he did not like things going in the wrong hands. He first took out the key and then suddenly asked Nico, "Why do you need it?" "My two friends Bryan and Ryan had to do a task which Big Billy gave them. To complete it, we need the key to the room. This is now the last remaining room," Nico replied. "You think I'll fall for the trick. Naughty boys.

Maybe, after all, it might be you stealing the trophies," the receptionist said.

The boys did not know what to do, but suddenly Nico got an idea, and he whispered to the boys. Nico's plan was to go to Mr. Atkinson's table, push his name tag off his table, tell him that Big Billy had stolen it, and then run to Big Billy to warn him. Thereafter, as per plan, Bryan would take the key and reach the door of the winners' room. Nico started executing the plan and faked a sneeze in front of the receptionist. With his hand, he pushed the name tag and made it fall on the floor. Nico told Mr Atkinson, "I think Big Billy has stolen your name tag. I saw him at your desk just a few minutes ago."

Nico was much faster than the receptionist to reach Big Billy first and warn him. Nico went to the room where Big Billy usually was, and to his relief, he was there. He told Big Billy, "Mr Atkinson is coming to you, and he is angry."

Meanwhile, the important part of the plan to get the key worked splendidly. Bryan opened the drawer and took the key to the winners' room. The boys knew the trouble Big Billy would get into, and they heard Mr Atkinson rudely ordering Big Billy to give his name tag back.

Meanwhile, Bryan went to the door of winners' room number 5 and waited for Nico. After two minutes, Nico came and asked Bryan to pass the key. Bryan handed over the key to Nico and requested Nico to open the door of the room of the winners.

As the boys opened the door, they were shocked and could not believe what they saw. The trophies were missing!

The boys carefully looked at the window of the room, and it was closed. The boys were surprised. Ryan said, "How is this possible?" Bryan added, "Impossible. How can the trophies vanish from the closed room?" Meanwhile, Nico seemed intently looking at something.

Just then, the boys saw the receptionist, Mr Atkinson, come into the room. Mr Atkinson, shouted, "Where are the trophies? Missing? So, you boys are the thieves. And Nico also."

Nico had a quick glance at something on the floor of the winners' room. It was a key. Nico grabbed it and quickly put it inside his pocket.

The receptionist further added angrily, "You three come to the manager's room. I want to know the truth. Quickly come to Mr Boggs' room." Saying this, the receptionist took them to the manager Mr Boggs' room and handed them to the manager. The receptionist left the room while Mr Boggs locked his room from inside and started asking questions.

Outside the inn, Jack and Zack saw the two thieves escaping with the winners' trophies from the open window. Jack and Zack tried to follow them but were unable to catch the thieves. The thieves had a motorbike hidden in a corner outside the inn. They zoomed on the motorbike with both the trophies.

Jack and Zack rushed inside the inn to call Bryan and Ryan, thinking all four of them would try to go in the direction of the thieves. But both Bryan and Ryan were not in sight. Zack, feeling frustrated, told Jack, "We came in to call them. But Bryan and Ryan are not here. We have lost all chances to catch the thieves." Both the boys felt betrayed, sad, and angry. Jack and Zack then tried to look for Nico, who also wasn't there. They thought he might be in the kitchen. So, they asked some other waiter for two glasses of orange juice. They hoped Nico would come with the bill, but still there was no sign of Nico.

Jack and Zack had a big chance of catching the thieves, but were feeling sad for missing it. The thought of being betrayed by their friends, Ryan and Bryan, hurt them even more. Jack and Zack spoke together, "These are our trophies. So, it's our job to find them after all."

Meanwhile in the manager's room, the other two boys and Nico were there for more than an hour. Finally, Ryan said, "Let's call the police and let them find out who the thief is." Bryan added, "Great idea. I will call the police." Mr. Boggs suddenly cooled down and said, "I know you are the thieves, but I will leave you as you are the guests of our inn." The three boys immediately walked out of Mr Boggs' room.

Both Jack and Zack felt sad and decided to go back to their room. After some time, there was a knock on the door. Jack opened it and was surprised to see that there were Bryan and Ryan at the door. "Jack and Zack. I want to tell you something," Bryan said. Jack replied, "Why betrayers?" Ryan said, "Why are you calling us betrayers? You are the ones betraying us." Jack said, "Why didn't you both come down and help us catch the thieves." Bryan angrily said, "We were locked inside the manager's room." Jack applauded sarcastically and said, "Excuse of the century."

Bryan said, "It is actually true. Where do you think we were for the last forty-five minutes?"

Ryan calmly told both Jack and Zack, who were still angry, "Please relax and sit down, and we'll tell you the whole story slowly." Thereafter, Ryan narrated the series of events.

Jack and Zack also told the events, they had witnessed from outside.

Bryan said, "So, we finally know how trophies were stolen. Sadly, we could not catch the thieves."

Ryan finally mentioned, "I think the manager of this inn, Mr Boggs, is directly involved in stealing the trophies. He suddenly calmed down when we threatened to call the police."

Soon, Nico also came to their room. He said, handing over the key, "This is the key I found today in the winners' room. '*Dupli Key*' is written on it. I assume it means a duplicate key. Maybe the thieves dropped it. The thieves are gone now. You keep it."

Ryan smiled and said, "I will keep the key. Who knows where it belongs to? Maybe it might help us someday, if really the thieves had dropped it."

Zack added, "Today, there was lots of action. We still have some hope. Let's plan our next steps now."

Chapter - 8

A New Idea

The four boys woke up the following morning thinking about what to do next. Though they had seen the thieves, sadly, they could not catch them. The quadruplets had to think of an idea to finally catch the thieves.

The boys decided to tell the coach about the events of the previous day. The coach was not there at the inn the entire previous day, as he had gone for the coaches' annual conference. The coach was sitting in the café of the inn, slowly sipping tea from his cup. The boys went to him. The coach asked them, "What's the latest news? What happened yesterday?"

Ryan replied sadly, "Coach, we have come to talk to you about yesterday." The coach said excitedly, "So, what happened yesterday?"

Bryan said in a low voice, "No, we could not catch the thieves. But we saw how they were stealing." Ryan narrated all the events of the previous day to the coach.

"So, you couldn't catch the thieves," the coach said in a sad tone, after listening to what the boys had to say. He continued, "Now, what will you do?" The coach thought that the boys would say that they want to give up, but he was shocked when he heard them telling that they want to think of another plan. Jack said, "We will think of a plan." The coach smiled, "Wow! You guys don't give up."

The coach said to the boys, "Oh! I almost forgot to tell you that the day after tomorrow is the last final of the tennis tournament. Alright, you make a new plan. I am with you."

The boys went to their room to think about a new plan. Jack came up with an idea and said, "I think I've got a plan. In my view, we four should stay outside the inn to follow the thieves to where all the stolen trophies are." Zack said, "I think two of us should stay inside the inn, just like earlier. This is because if we all stay outside, then we won't be able to see if someone steals from inside." Finally, they agreed that all the four boys should be outside the building of the inn to observe the thieves stealing the trophies and thereafter following them as a group.

The boys kept discussing about various options to catch the thieves till it was lunch time. The boys were happy with an opportunity to catch the thieves and decided to have lunch at the inn. There were many varieties of food, including their favourite dishes. The boys had sausages with mashed potatoes and stir-fried vegetables. The food was so delicious that the plate was as clean as before eating. The four boys really loved the food.

The four boys decided to go and walk outside the inn and think more about their plan. The two pairs of twins pondered and pondered on the plan.

The boys were going to their room when Chris Wilson, the tennis coach, called them. He said, "Bryan and Ryan. Tomorrow is the one-day football tournament in London among the Walter family's private schools. There are four schools participating. Regent High School, Beacon High School, Palmers Green High School, and Wimbledon High School." The four boys were studying at Palmers Green High School. The coach further said, "I told my brother, Thomas, who is also in charge of the school football team, that you both are here. He will be here tomorrow early morning." Jack and Zack asked the coach if they could also accompany Bryan and Ryan. The coach said, "Yeah, why not and also note that the tournament is happening at Wimbledon High School."

Bryan and Ryan had completely forgotten about their football tournament, as they were busy discussing plans to catch the thieves. But how could they? They knew they were in the starting eleven of their school football team.

The boys quickly called a waiter and asked him for four cheese sandwiches. The sandwiches came in five minutes and they were consumed within minutes, as they were hungry walking outside for a long time. The boys retired early in order to be rested for the football tournament the following day.

Next day morning, just when the boys finished breakfast, they heard somebody call them. To their surprise, they could not find out who called them. There was only one man in the hall, whom they could not recognise. The man said, "I actually called you. You didn't recognise me? I am Thomas Wilson, your football coach. I just grew a beard and tied up my hair." "Oh, my deepest apologies, coach," Ryan smiled. The tennis coach's brother and football coach, Thomas Wilson, who had come to take the boys, said laughingly, "Good thing I got a big car, otherwise your friends would have been left back or would have to come in the boot of the car." The five of them went to the car along with another person, who was Coach Thomas' friend and was driving the car. It was a six-seater car. The four boys sat at the back, while Coach Thomas Wilson and his friend were in the front.

During the car drive, the football coach explained the team formation and tactics to Bryan and Ryan. The proposed formation was 3-2-4-1. The keeper was their tall friend, Frank. The substitute keeper was their other tall friend, Dennis. The defence consisted of the twins, Harry and Kevin, and their third mate in defence was James, who had recently joined their school. The defence midfielders, Michael and Mathew, were good friends of Bryan and Ryan. The wingers were Bryan and Ryan, while the attacking midfielders were Percy and Peter. Peter and Percy were Bryan and Ryan's best friends, after Jack and Zack. The lone striker was Jason. Bryan, Ryan, and Jason teamed up really well.

The main tactic was playing possession football and feeding the ball to the wingers, who would cut in or cross to the striker, Jason, in the middle. The football coach told Ryan and Bryan, "The format of the tournament is like you are directly playing a semi-final. The game is for one and a half hours. I know we only have twelve players, and I know you two have the most stamina. Now, in this game we are going to keep possession of the ball. You shouldn't tire yourselves, but if you don't give your hundred percent we'll be out of the tournament in no time." Ryan said, "And coach, one more point about our opponent is that they don't even try to tackle unless you enter their box." The coach said, "Oh, you know whom we are facing." The boys said, "Beacon High School."

The boys reached the football stadium. At that time, the earlier football game between Wimbledon and Regent was about to start.

Ryan and Bryan went to the dressing room and met their football teammates. Jack and Zack sat with the football coach on the side just outside the football field and ready to cheer their friends.

"We've got our jersey numbers," one of the football players, Percy, said. He further elaborated the jersey numbers of the team players, "Frank has 1, James has 2, Harry 3, Kevin 4, Michael 5, Matthew 6, Peter 8, me 10, and Jason 9. Ryan, I think you are 11, Bryan you're 7, and Dennis is 12. It suits him, twelfth man having number 12."

Bryan and Ryan changed into their jerseys along with other team players and started warming up. The team was discussing about the previous game, and someone said, "Which is a better football team – Wimbledon or Regent?" Percy said, "Wimbledon football team is clearly better. They will thrash the other team." The other boys also thought the Wimbledon football team would win. The coach came and told the boys, "Think about your match. Not others." The boys again started practising by playing some passes. The twelve boys played beautiful passes. Everyone in the team had a good pace while the keepers were required to stay at the goalposts and stop the goals.

After completing the practice session of passing the ball, the coach divided the twelve boys' team into six vs six practice match. One team was of attackers and attacking midfielders called '*Attackers*', while the second team was of defenders and defending midfielders called '*Defenders*'.

The practice game was initially equally balanced with attacking moves by *Attackers* while *Defenders* blocking almost every attack. A long shot into the opponent's goal put the *Defenders* ahead with the score of 1-0.

The *Attackers* had to quickly come back into the game. At that moment, *Attackers* team's striker, Percy, got the ball and saw his opponent team-mate, Kevin, furiously running towards him. Percy sprinted forward with the ball to the opponent's goal line and quickly passed to his team-mate, Bryan, who cleverly continued dribbling. At that moment, it was Bryan from the *Attackers* team vs James from the *Defenders* team. Bryan suddenly spotted his team-mate and his twin brother, Ryan, who was also making a run towards the opponent's goal. Bryan smartly chipped the ball over to Ryan, who controlled the ball well. Ryan quickly shot into the goal and levelled the match at 1-1.

The coach suddenly announced, "Next goal wins." Both the teams quickly regrouped to go for the winning goal.

From the centre start, James of the *Defenders* team took an unexpected long shot all the way into the top corner of *Attackers* goal. The *Attackers* goalkeeper, Dennis, flung himself towards the ball and somehow managed to save the goal. The goalkeeper smartly made a long shot to his team-mate, Bryan, standing in the opponent's half. Bryan saw his team-mate, Peter, unmarked close to *Defenders* team's goal and passed the ball to him. Peter cleverly received the ball and scored the goal easily. The score was 2-1 to the *Attackers* team. The coach blew the whistle. The *Attackers* team players jumped in joy, as they had fought back from 0-1 down to win 2-1.

After playing their own practice match, the boys took some rest. In the meantime, they heard the final whistle of the ongoing match of the football tournament. The score was 3-1 for the Wimbledon football team.

Finally, it was time for the Palmers Green High School football team's match. The coach decided that Bryan should be the captain of the team. The captain led their team to the field and then went for the toss. Bryan won and chose to start.

From the moment the game started, Bryan's school team was dominant. Within a few minutes of starting the game, Bryan crossed the ball and Jason headed it towards the goal but just missed the goal. Finally, in the thirty-ninth minute, the ball was passed to Bryan, who dribbled past two defenders and crossed it to his team-mate, Percy, who shot the ball towards the opponent's goal. The shot was stopped by the *Defenders*, but the ball rebounded to Bryan, who positioned it for Peter, who finally shot into the goal. Bryan's team had many more chances, but couldn't score more goals, despite playing well. The score ended 1-0 for Bryan's team. Bryan and Ryan's team was in the finals! The boys decided to rest after the match, and in the meantime, watched the third-fourth place game. The game went to a penalty shoot-out. The winner was the Regent School team, who won five to three on penalty shoot-outs.

The teams prepared themselves for the finals. Bryan led the Palmers Green team to the football pitch. He lost the toss, but still his team got the opportunity to start the game, as the opponent chose the goal side. The final match was full of action. In the twelfth minute, the opponent team, Wimbledon School, took the lead with a goal. In the thirty-first minute, Bryan dribbled well and set-up for Peter, who scored. The scores were level at 1-1. In the eighty-fourth minute, the Palmers Green team got a freekick. Bryan, Ryan, and Peter were choosing who would take the freekick. The Palmers Green team boys had a plan. Ryan took the kick, but only softly passed the ball to Bryan, who only stopped it. Peter suddenly ran from behind and kicked an unstoppable shot into the goal. The opponents never expected this. Palmers Green were in the lead with 2-1.

In ninety plus two minutes added time, Palmers Green got a corner. Peter whipped it in, but the opponent's defender cleared it. Frank came up to half pitch and tried to kick the ball, but he could not connect well. Instead, the ball went to the opponent's striker, who ran towards Palmer Green's goal. Bryan ran as fast as he could but missed the ball by a second. The ball had entered the Palmer Green's box, and the opponent's striker was about to shoot when Bryan dived and kicked the ball, and the striker fell over his leg. The referee was at the half pitch, and he thought it was a foul by Bryan, and thus showed him a yellow card and also gave a penalty to the opponents. Ryan protested, but he could not do anything. The referee also gave Ryan and Frank a yellow card each for protesting. The goalkeeper, Frank, was substituted by Palmers Green for Dennis, as Dennis was better at stopping penalties. Dennis knew that most right-footers shoot towards their left. He guessed correctly and dived to his right and stopped the penalty.

Soon, the final whistle blew, and Palmers Green were the champions. Their captain Bryan had won the most assists award, and the best player and the highest goal scorer was Peter. The team celebrated along with Jack, Zack, and the coach. The team then went to their school, where they continued their celebrations.

The players of the Palmers Green Football team slept early in their school's hostel, as they were exhausted. The team woke up early the next day, and the four boys went back to Coalsy Inn to continue their efforts of catching the trophy thieves. They reached Coalsy Inn and thanked the football coach for driving them back, ate brunch and read books for a while.

All the four boys had free time till evening before the winners came, so they decided to go to a local fair. At around 1:00 p.m., the four boys left the inn for the fair.

The idea of going to the fair was very exciting. So, they still decided to go to the fair even though it was drizzling. The fair had many games stalls, and food stalls, and this one had even a large book stall. First, the boys played darts. Then they went to drink a hot chocolate each from a food stall. After that, the four of them went to the bookstall that they were most attracted to. The boys found a book each and read it for some time, and then ate a croissant each, and finally excitedly went back to the inn along with the books they got from the bookstall at the fair.

Back at the inn, the boys chatted for a while on their important plan for the evening of catching thieves and then Jack said in a serious voice, "Those thieves had a motorcycle. They are much faster than us." "Yes, you are right, but we don't know what we can do," Ryan said. Jack said, "I saw them going fast on their motorcycle on that road after stealing the trophies."

Bryan explained, "Thanks, Jack. We know they'll go on that same road next time also when they steal the trophies. It has been raining today. While the roads will dry in some time, the puddles will remain. There is a big puddle on the road at the start of that path just outside the inn, and there are many more on the road. Also, many vehicles do not use this road. This is only a small stretch of road which leads to a tiny forest area." Ryan further added, "Good thing there are many small depressions on the road. As they are lower than the road, the muddy water will gather there, and with the help of that, we can follow their tyre marks. Also, hardly any vehicles use the road thieves took last time." "It'll work out, and I'm sure of it. These puddles will surely help us," Jack agreed.

Chapter - 9

A Desperate Attempt

Jack, Zack, Bryan and Ryan had to wait for the latest winners to come to the inn before executing their plan. This was their last chance, as it was the last final of this tournament. The quadruplets were desperate to catch the thieves.

The boys waited in their room for the winners to arrive. They played a game of Ludo in their room keeping the door of their room open. The game was to show others that they are playing, but they were actually focussing on the winners' room. The boys started playing, but their game was stopped midway when the tennis tournament winners reached their room at the inn. The boys quickly stopped their game and went down to the dining hall. They knew the winners would still be changing, so they waited patiently in the dining hall for the winners to come down. Suddenly, Zack remembered and told the rest, "How can we see the tyre marks if it gets dark? We need a torch or something. Does anyone have a torch?" Bryan replied, "I do. I'll go and get it." He went up and searched for it in Ryan's bag, which he thought was his. Bryan became sad and was about to go back when he suddenly remembered it was Ryan's bag, not his. He finally found the torch in his bag and ran down happily.

After some time still waiting for the winners, Ryan said, "We are lucky. Today was the last final of the tournament. We thought the day before yesterday was the last final." All the others agreed. Jack saw that all of them were feeling thirsty, as it was humid due to the rain earlier in the day. So, he went to get them each a glass of water and on his way, he met the tennis coach. The tennis coach asked surprisingly, "What are you doing here? Shouldn't you be capturing the thieves?" "Coach, I am here to get three glasses of water," said Jack. The coach replied, "Jack, you only have two small hands. How will you hold three glasses?" Jack asked, "Coach, I was just thinking about if you could also come and help us in finding the thieves?" "I would like to come, and I'll also hold one glass for you," the coach said.

"So, what's your plan?" the coach asked while walking with Jack. "Coach, our plan is to follow the thieves once they steal the trophies. We can also follow the tyre marks of the bike of the thieves, as the road in many places has puddles. The thieves would have to go through these puddles," Jack replied. "Yes, it looks like a good plan and that road is not too long to follow," the coach agreed. The coach put on a wig so that nobody could recognise him, and he could help the boys in catching the thieves.

When Jack came along with the coach in the dining hall, the rest of the boys were angry at Jack. Ryan was first to say to Jack, "Whom have you brought along? Have you forgotten it's our mystery? Maybe this new guy is part of the thieves' gang or maybe he'll take all the glory for himself." The coach said, "Hey, I'm not a part of their gang." He was interrupted by Ryan, who said, "No, we do not need any outsiders." The coach said jokingly, "In fact, I'm the one who should be the leader of your team bossing you around. Not you, Ryan."

Ryan said to Jack with a big surprise, "You even told him our names. Was that necessary?" Jack said, "Actually, I didn't tell him; he already knows our names." Ryan was totally confused and said, "Oh, really if so, then who is he?" "He is our tennis coach, Chris Wilson. He has specially come to help us," Jack said, laughing. The coach said, "It took so long for you to recognise me, Ryan? I thought you would surely recognise me." Ryan was really apologetic and said, "Sorry coach for not recognising you. It's so nice to be with you now." The coach smiled, "Don't worry. Just having some fun. I am always with you all."

After all the fun, the coach joined the boys in their mission of finding the missing trophies. The boys took their positions, as per their plan. All the boys and the coach hid just outside the building of the inn in such a way that the thieves could not see them. At the same time, they could quietly observe the thieves entering and exiting the winners' room through the outside window.

They had only one last chance to recover their trophies!

After around five minutes, they saw the same two thieves they had seen the last time. One was short and well-built, while the other was tall and lean but seemed to possess the same power as the other, if not more.

The boys were able to observe the thieves opening the closed window from outside. The way the thieves had opened the window was a genius' work. The boys admired it, even though the thieves had stolen their trophy as well. Even Chris Wilson, the coach, admired it. The boys named it ANTS, which was short form for 'A New Technology of Scissors'. The ANTS was a scissor-like instrument and had two hook-like things with a corner to grab onto the bolt and pull it down. In this way, thieves could then go through the window with ease. One main reason was that the windows did not have grills. Coalsy was an old and famous inn in one end of London and did not have grills on the windows just like all old inns.

After the thieves again successfully opened the window of the winners' room from outside with their special 'ANTS' instrument, they went into the winners' room through the open window. It looked like they had a hard time finding the trophies, as they took a long time inside the winners' room. The boys quietly watched them from outside the inn.

After the thieves found the winners' trophies, they came out from the open window, and went on their motorcycle, just like last time. The thieves rode very fast, not caring about the puddles of water on the road. The boys' idea was working. The boys, along with the coach, ran after the thieves. It was still evening so they could see the road and the tyre marks. Still, Bryan turned on his torch. The boys could see the tyre marks glistening on the road in the light of the torch. The boys followed the marks until it started to drizzle. They knew the rain would erase the tyre marks, so the four boys along with the coach ran as fast as they could. Jack had a feeling that if they did not run fast, they would not be able to see where the tyre marks would end. The boys and the coach made all efforts to run fast. They ran until they could see nothing except a small cottage, which seemed like no one had used it for many years.

The boys searched around the cottage and behind the trees, but they couldn't find anything or anyone. The boys decided to check inside the cottage. The four boys, along with the coach, went to the door. The five of them were surprised to find that the door was locked. Bryan said, "What shall we do? How can we enter inside? We need to enter somehow."

Suddenly, Ryan remembered the key Nico had found in the winners' room at the inn. The key which had *'Dupli key'* written on it. Ryan said, "Does that key belong to the door of this cottage? But I do not have it now. It's in our room." Others screamed, "Let's quickly get it."

Zack was ready to get the key but he didn't fully remember the way back to the inn. While running after the thieves, the boys and the coach had quickly followed the tyre marks, fearing rain would wipe them, without paying much attention to the surroundings. With the recent rain, there would not be any marks visible on the road. Hence, it was difficult to reach back to the inn. They had to somehow find the way back quickly to the inn and again back to the abandoned cottage. Ryan said, "Don't you guys remember we only took one left turn and one right turn? Any recollection?" The coach said, "I remember we took our first turn after we passed the yellow flowers, and I think it was a left." Zack said, "I remember where we took the right turn, and now coach has told where we have to take the left turn. Ryan, if you tell me where is the key, I'll go and get it. You all stay here in case thieves come back."

"I left the key on the table in our room," said Ryan.

Chapter - 10

The Last Chance

Zack was going all alone back towards the inn with his torch to get the *'Dupli Key'*. All of them were hoping that this key would open the cottage door and they would find the stolen trophies inside. This was their last chance.

Zack ran as fast as he could. He came to the place where he had taken the right turn. Before turning, he saw if he was in the right place or not. It was the correct place. To his right was a huge oak tree, which he had seen on the left side while coming. He took the right and ran for what seemed like forever. The torch was kept in his pocket, so he could run faster. It was kept in such a way that he could see where he was running.

Finally, Zack saw the yellow flowers from where the coach had told them they had earlier taken a left. From there, he then took a right and carried on till he could finally see the inn. He still ran as fast as he could because he wanted to get the key and see what was inside the cottage. Zack only slowed down and decided to walk the last stretch instead of running. He saw that the inn was shining beautifully and admired the beauty of the inn while walking. Then he remembered that he had to get the key to the rest of the team as soon as possible. He started to run again. When he reached the entrance of the inn, a man was coming out while Zack was running inside. Zack tried his best not to hit the man, but he could not avoid it. He hit him and they both fell. Zack fell on top of the man. He got up and apologised. The man didn't say anything to Zack, because he knew Zack didn't mean anything bad and he was just a kid after all.

Zack also ran inside the inn, and when he opened the door, he saw a room attendant cleaning his room. The manager, Mr Graham Boggs, was standing next to the room attendant. When the manager saw Zack, the manager suddenly praised the person cleaning the room, "Bravo, you're cleaning just like I told you to." Mr Boggs said to Zack, "Oh Zack, you've come. I was just asking him to clean your room well." Zack was very surprised and replied, "Oh, thank you, Sir."

Zack did not see the key on the table. He understood Mr. Boggs had taken the *'Dupli Key'* and was quickly going out of the room.

The manager then walked around the inn, seeing if everything was in place or not. He told his head supervisor, "Hey Gary, take care of the inn for me. I'll just be going to take a bath. I was supervising the painting work outside and need to clean myself." Gary said, "Yes sir."

Thereafter, Mr. Boggs went towards his room, unlocked the door, and then suddenly remembered something. He went to the hall, and by that time, Zack had already made a plan. Zack quietly went inside the manager's room and hid in a corner behind a large cupboard. The manager had a large room with many cupboards. Zack waited for Mr. Boggs to come back to his room.

The manager had actually gone to the head supervisor, Gary, and told him, "A special guest is coming here. I'll wait for a few minutes, and then I'll go, if she doesn't come. Then you will have to welcome her and tell her I will be there in a few minutes. But do not tell why." Gary asked, "Sir, but why?" "She'll think that the manager of a famous inn doesn't welcome important guests like her. It would not be nice for the inn. You just tell her I'm in my room signing some very important papers, and I have asked you not to disturb me for just five to ten minutes. Just remember to mention the words 'very important papers'. Let her think I have important work. My guests need to think I am a manager, who personally welcomes the guests and who is also dedicated to his work. I want people to think I am a great manager –

dedicated and pleasant," Mr. Boggs said. Gary said smilingly, "Sure sir."

Zack was waiting for the manager to come back to his room, and it seemed forever waiting for him.

The manager, Mr Boggs, finally came back to his room and locked his door from inside and went to the washroom after leaving a key on the key rack. Zack thought it must be the '*Dupli Key*' he wanted. He was excited but decided to wait until he heard the sound of the shower. He waited for around two minutes, and then he went to get the key. He saw it was on the rack but kept on the highest shelf. Zack was a bit short for his age, and even when he jumped, he couldn't reach the key. He decided to do something quickly. He wanted some kind of a long rod.

Zack looked on the table in the manager's room and saw a calendar, a writing pad, a file of papers, a stand which had a stapler, scissors and three pens. He decided to take the big calendar and jumped to get the key. First, he jumped, but it didn't work. After many attempts, he finally got the key. He silently opened the door of the manager's room. He quietly went out, closed the door, and ran.

Zack knew he had wasted a lot of time, and the others would be waiting for him. He was tired and very thirsty, so he drank a glass of water, and then he decided to go to the old cottage. He took his torch and started running. He thought others would also be hungry. On the way back, he went to the nearest bakery and quickly got a box of ten doughnuts. Thereafter, Zack ran straight and then took a left, where he saw the yellow flowers. He continued on this path until he saw a huge tree. After running for a long time, there was no cottage in sight. He realised he was on the wrong path. Zack quickly retraced his steps till the place where he had taken the left turn. After some time, he reached the same oak tree and then he ran and finally came back to the boys at the cottage. Bryan said, "You finally came. It's almost midnight now." Zack was shocked and asked, "What, really, it took four hours." Bryan said, "No, I'm just joking, it's just 8:37 p.m."

"I got ten doughnuts for the five of us, two doughnuts for each of us, thinking all would be hungry," said Zack. The boys almost shouted at Zack for wasting time to get the doughnuts but realised that they were hungry. The four boys were hungry and very quickly finished their share of the doughnuts, while the coach also quickly ate his share and enjoyed it. After they had finished eating, they kept the empty box in the bag and kept it on a rock.

After eating, when Zack put his hand in his pocket to get the key, it was not there. He was shocked! He had a feeling it would have come out of his pocket while running back towards the cottage from the inn. He told the rest that they should search on the path that he had come back on. He, along with the rest, searched for the key and it took a while as it was dark. They finally found the key on the path close to the cottage, shining in the darkness. They happily took the key and started walking back to the cottage. While walking,

Jack asked Zack, "Why did you take thirty-seven minutes?" Zack said, "It's a long story." Zack quickly narrated the whole story.

The boys took the '*Dupli Key*' hoping it would work. Ryan quickly inserted the key in the main door, but it did not open. The boys were very dejected. Ryan took out the key, and this time he slowly put the key in the lock and turned it with more pressure. Initially, nothing happened, but then suddenly he heard a sound and the lock opened. All the boys jumped with joy. It was an old lock, and it needed some extra effort to open it.

The quadruplets and the coach decided to go inside the cottage and search. Zack took out the torch and opened the main door of the cottage. After opening the door, they found out that it had two rooms and a lobby. Ryan said, "Bryan and I will check the lobby, Jack and Zack the room on the left, and coach the room on the right." Jack joked, "Aye, aye, captain." Bryan said, "We are not pirates." Jack said, "I know. I was just joking."

The boys started to search. They looked everywhere but couldn't find anything. The only thing which was found was a cigarette butt. The boys decided to search again together, hoping to find something. After some time, Jack asked Bryan, "Do you know anything about when the thieves will come, Bryan?" Bryan gave no reply. Jack again said, "Any idea, Bryan?" Ryan said, "Bryan, don't prank us." Suddenly, they heard a sound. While walking, Ryan suddenly slipped and fell into a hole in the floor and landed with a loud thud. Bryan said, "Rest of you, come here. Let's see where Ryan has fallen into." The rest came down through the opening one by one, and then the boys started exploring there. It was like a hidden basement. The boys searched for some time and found the trophies!

The boys had finally found the trophies! There were screams of happiness, and all the boys were jumping with joy.

The boys started counting and found a total of ten trophies! All from the same tournament. These were of the winners of the five doubles' finals of the Kent County Centenary Tournament.

Zack found his trophy and shouted excitedly, "This trophy is mine." Jack rushed and held his trophy and said, "This is my trophy." Both Jack and Zack again posed as winners holding their trophies and others clapping for them.

Their happiness suddenly came to an end when the coach told them, "We are stuck here. There seems to be no way out. The hole in the ceiling from where we came down is too high to reach. There is no ladder or table here for us to climb up."

Jack got so angry that he kicked the wall. Zack just sat and observed that a small squirrel had come from a corner of the basement. He went to the corner and saw that there was a door, but it was not opening. Zack told his observation to the rest. The team together pushed the door open, but it still did not open. The lock was jammed. The coach and the boys together pushed it very hard, and the door finally opened, leading into a passage. There suddenly seemed some hope to get out of the basement.

Ryan first went out through the passage and signalled others to follow. The coach saw a big bag in the basement. He put eight trophies in the big bag, which he held along with Bryan. Jack held his trophy while Zack held his. The passage led them outside of the cottage from the back door.

The boys were very happy and decided to go back to their school with all the trophies. The coach said, "No. Before going, we need to also catch the thieves."

They kept the trophies on a rock outside the cottage behind a large tree so that nobody could see them. They decided to wait for the thieves to catch them whenever they would return back. All of them were so tired that they fell asleep, as it was late night by then. They dozed off on the grass right next to the trophies.

Chapter - 11

The Reason for Stealing

The boys were woken up early the next morning, just when the morning sun came into their eyes. The boys, along with the coach, had slept the previous night outside the old cottage while waiting for the thieves to come back. In the morning, the boys saw that the cottage was the only one around and surrounded by beautiful orchards with lots of fruits.

Zack went in search of water and found one spring not too far away. He drank some water from the spring. The water was crystal-clear with a sweet taste. He went back to the rest and told them about the spring. They all went and drank the crystal-clear sweet water and came back. The boys, along with the coach, decided to keep waiting outside the cottage for the thieves. Bryan glanced at his watch and said, "It's almost six. I think we woke up at five forty-five."

The coach got the idea of eating berries and fruits from the adjoining orchard. The cottage was in the middle of an orchard with various fruits. The boys thought it was a good idea that Jack and Zack would collect the strawberries, Bryan and Ryan would get the apples, and the coach would get the cherries. Only two people would go at any time, while others would look out for the thieves. The boys searched in the orchard so that they could find the fruits. After some time, they collected the fruits and came back to the place where they had kept the trophies. They saw that Jack and Zack got fifteen strawberries, Bryan and Ryan got five apples, and the coach got fifteen cherries. The boys and the coach took three strawberries each, an apple each and three cherries each. The cherries were extremely sweet, the strawberries were delicious, and so were the apples. The boys happily ate the fruits. They were wondering how long they should wait or go with the trophies to the police station.

The boys knew that it was likely that the thieves would come back to the cottage to get all the trophies. The coach wanted to know why they had stolen the trophies. The coach said, "We need more boys to help us catch the thieves. I am sure they will come back to get the trophies." Ryan said, "We can call the players of the football team from our school. The same team Bryan and I are part of. It's not very far away." Bryan decided to go to their school, and the other three decided to stay back and wait for the thieves while guarding the trophies.

The plan was that Bryan would go with the coach in his car. The coach and Bryan walked towards the inn and then went in the coach's car. When they reached the school, Bryan thought that their teammates would be asleep. He was right. One by one, he woke up some of his team mates. They woke up and he then told them the whole story, and all the other boys got ready within minutes. Five boys, along with Bryan and the coach, reached the cottage in the coach's car. Finally, there were nine boys at the old cottage to catch the thieves. The coach said, "The thieves haven't come back yet." The ten of them, including the coach, hid behind bushes which surrounded the cottage and decided that when the thieves would come back, they could capture the thieves.

The boys waited for one hour, and then suddenly they saw the two thieves coming back to the cottage. The ten of them from all sides surrounded the two thieves.

The thieves were young boys around fifteen years old. Zack shouted at the thieves, "You thieves. We will take you to the police station."

The thieves were scared and said, "Don't send us to jail. It was not our idea. We were just asked to do it." The boys asked them to tell as to why they were stealing the trophies. One of the thieves told, "Our father is severely ill, and we need money for his treatment. This is my brother Kasper, and I am Jasper. We are good athletes and good at tennis too. We asked the mayor, who was in charge, if we could participate in Kent County's Centenary tournament because we knew we could win it. Then, as winners, we could ask for some money from somebody, or somebody could sponsor us. We need money for the treatment of our father. The mayor's office told us that our town, Fordwich, could not participate in this tournament, even though it's part of the county of Kent. Fordwich is not part of the list of towns approved for this tournament, as our town is too small to be considered. Hence, we could not participate in this tennis tournament."

One of the thieves, Kasper, further added, "After the rejection of any possibility to participate in the tournament, we sadly went back to the hospital. One man met us at the hospital and told us he could help us. We thought he was a kind man and told him our story. Turns out we met the wrong person. He asked us to steal the ten trophies, and then he would pay for the treatment of our father. The offer was very tempting, but we didn't want to do it. The temptation was just too much. We really wanted our father to be fine, so we agreed. He told us the plan, including how to open the window. We stole five times, and now he has asked us to give the trophies to him after which he will give us the money. While we have stolen the trophies, we still did not feel like giving them to him. That is why we did not take all the trophies to him last night. We still do not have the money, as we have not given the trophies to him."

The other thief, Jasper, further added, "Jack and Zack. Yours were the first set of trophies we had stolen, followed by trophies of four other doubles' winners. Total ten trophies of five doubles tournaments."

The coach said, "Who is this person teaching you to do wrong deeds?" One of the thieves, Kasper, replied, "He is Earl Grayson." The coach replied, "Aah. Earl Grayson. He wants to make the mayor look bad. He just lost the election of the mayor. He lost it to the current mayor."

Zack asked the thieves, "Who all were helping you in Coalsy Inn?" Jasper replied, "The manager, Mr. Graham Boggs, was the person who was there to help us. He has one more person helping us." Jack immediately said, "The other person would be the same person who wanted our room." Zack asked surprisingly, "Why would Mr Boggs help in this?" Kasper replied, "We don't know the full story. But it seems Mr Boggs has taken some money from Earl Grayson, who has somehow forced Mr Boggs to help in stealing the trophies."

Jasper said nervously, "Will we go to jail?" The coach said, "No, you're not going to jail if you cooperate with us." Jasper continued, "Now I understand. His dirty plan is working. Today is the day the mayor is supposed to give the trophies to the winners. And he will not be able to give it. Only two of you are here."

The coach said to Jasper and Kasper, "Thanks for reminding us. Now, come with us to the mayor and tell him the whole story. Regarding the money for your father, we will request the mayor for help. I know him well, and we can seek his help. We also have to send messages to other winners." The two boys, who now trusted them, agreed to do what the coach told them.

The four boys understood that Jasper and Kasper were misguided and pardoned them. Jasper and Kasper said, "We will go with you to the police station or the mayor's office. Whatever you say."

Zack said, "Let's go to the police station and then to the mayor. We also need to get ready."

The coach said, "Let's first go to the police station along with Jasper and Kasper. We need to inform other winners. Then, I will take you to the school to get ready for the evening." The quadruplets shouted in excitement, "Yes, coach."

Chapter - 12

The Prize Ceremony

The boys and the coach rushed to the county of Kent's main police station along with the two thieves and the trophies. The boys told the policemen the whole story, and the policemen were astounded. The boys requested help to send messages to the other winners. The policeman asked, "Where do you want them to come?" The coach said, "Please send them to the Speakers' Corner in Hyde Park and tell them to wear their best clothes, preferably a suit."

Both the thieves, Jasper and Kasper, said sorry and asked for forgiveness. The police told them not to worry and to accompany them to meet the mayor.

The coach told the boys, "Let me take four of you to the school so that you can get ready.

After that, let's go straight to Hyde Park with the trophies. The mayor would be there for the event."

All the boys quickly changed into their best suits and got ready for the prize distribution ceremony. Bryan had worn a red coat, red tie, and a white shirt. Ryan got dressed in a brown coat, with a brown tie on a white shirt. Jack had worn a black coat, a black tie, and a white shirt, while Zack wore a dark blue coat, a dark blue tie, and a white shirt. The four of them wore different colours of shoes to match their suits.

On the way to Hyde Park, the boys picked up their waiter friend, Nico, from the Coalsy Inn to join them. Nico also quickly got dressed up and accompanied them.

The five boys, along with the coach, reached the Speakers' Corner in Hyde Park along with all the trophies well in time. The mayor was meeting a few people in the audience. They went to the mayor and gave him all the trophies, and the coach told him the whole story. The mayor, Paul Radley, was a very nice person. He smiled without saying anything while asking his staff to keep all the trophies next to the stage.

The mayor was astounded by the actions of Earl Grayson. The mayor understood that it was all done by Earl Grayson to make him look bad at the centenary event. The mayor knew it was the 'Centenary Year' celebrations of the county, and prize distribution was a key event. He knew that Earl Grayson would make all efforts to embarrass him. After some time, the other winners also reached the venue and were confused, as they did not have the trophies.

In the front row, Earl Grayson was seated and was smiling thinking there were no trophies to honour the winners.

Soon, the centenary ceremony began. A person from the mayor's office went up to the microphone and started saying, "Good evening to all of you. We are happy to start the ceremony. Though this tournament was for the county of Kent, we have specially organised the prize ceremony in Hyde Park, London, as we were looking for a prestigious place to give the awards. Also, the tennis finals took place very close to this place. The mayor will be giving the trophies of the Kent County Centenary Tennis Tournament."

The mayor smilingly walked up to the stage, while Earl Grayson's smile suddenly vanished. The mayor said, "Good evening to one and all. I am proud to stand here to begin celebrations of another centenary of our county. To begin with, we will give the awards to the winners of the *Centenary Tennis Tournament.*"

The mayor further said, "So now I am going to call upon the boys who have won the trophies in this *Centenary Tennis Tournament.*" He called out all the names of the winners and, one by one, gave everyone the trophy. Surprisingly, Jack and Zack were not called.

After the trophies were given, the mayor asked everyone to be silent and started speaking, "I have to make one important announcement. Earl Grayson got all these trophies stolen, so that we have a loss of face at this centenary celebration. The police will take up this case further. The good news is that we got all the trophies with us. The same trophies we have distributed just now." Everyone in the audience was shocked and screamed, "Shame."

The mayor continued, "A few brave boys managed to get all the trophies back, not just theirs but of all the winners. It was not the police, but four smart boys. Also, few others helped them." The audience started clapping and asked, "Who are the boys?"

The mayor said, "I will now call them and award them. First, I will call the winners of under-13 Doubles' champions – Jack and Zack Pietersen." Jack and Zack proudly took their trophies from the mayor. The mayor asked them to wait on the stage. Next, he said, "Now I call Bryan and Ryan Mason." Both the boys rushed on the stage. The mayor said, "Dear Friends. These four boys found their trophies and also of all the other winners. Let's give them a standing ovation for their fantastic work." The entire audience stood up to clap. The mayor said, "These four boys will get a special award from me soon." The audience clapped even more.

The mayor continued, "There were two people who helped them, and I need to also thank them." The mayor called out Nicolas Allen. Nico walked up to the stage and shook hands with the mayor. Nico could not believe he was with the mayor. The mayor finally said, "I also want to thank my friend and the boys' tennis coach, Chris Wilson, for guiding all the boys. This would not have been possible without him." The coach walked up and warmly shook hands with the mayor.

The mayor said, "Before I finish this award ceremony, I also wanted to mention that there are two boys, Kasper and Jasper. They stole the trophies, but have understood their mistake. I pardon them. Also, I will look into their town being included in the tennis tournament next year and will also try to help their father."

After coming down from the stage, Jack and Zack called Bryan and Ryan and said, "This is the trophy for all four of us. We never thought we would have our trophies for the centenary celebrations from the mayor."

All four boys, Jack, Zack, Bryan, and Ryan, hugged each other and said, "What a wonderful adventure for four of us."

The boys sang together:

We are not just the champions and won the trophies.

We also solved the mystery of the vanishing trophies.

www.ingramcontent.com/pod-product-compliance
Lightning Source LLC
Chambersburg PA
CBHW021959150726
47990CB00002B/517